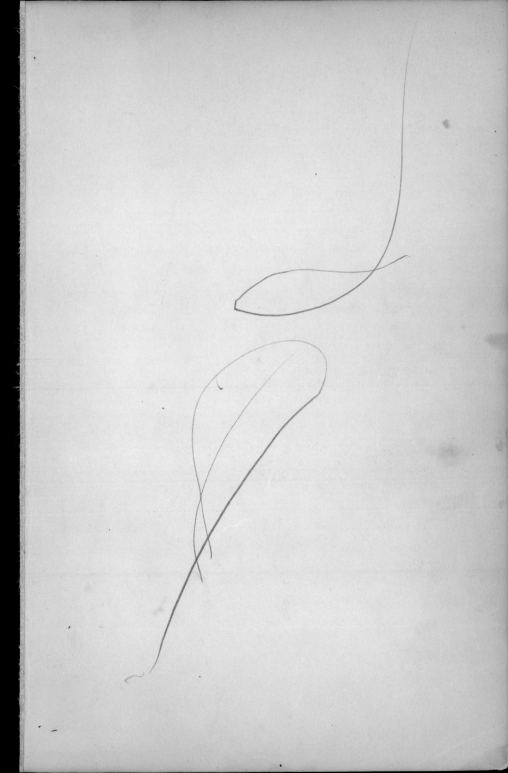

WILD GEESE FLYING

Also by Cornelia Meigs

WILD GEESE FLYING

BY CORNELIA MEIGS

Illustrated by Charles Geer

THE MACMILLAN COMPANY, NEW YORK

© THE MACMILLAN COMPANY 1957

A shorter version appeared serially in *Jack and Jill,* © The Curtis Publishing Company 1955, 1956.

Library of Congress catalog card number: 57-5972

First Printing

PRINTED IN THE UNITED STATES OF AMERICA

Contents

TO
JAMES
FROM
HIS AUNT

CHAPTER ONE

The Running Deer

The woods were full of wind that morning, of dry, warm, October wind, which sent the leaves twirling down from the gold and scarlet birch and maple trees. They swept all around Dick Milton as he walked forward steadily; they did not rustle and crackle under his feet for they were not yet dry enough, but drifted into layers that were thick and soft as he pushed through them. The mountainside was steep, and it was quiet and empty; it was here for him to explore quite by himself.

"Don't go too far," his mother had said, "and if you

feel for a minute that you are lost—and anyone can get lost on a mountain—just walk downhill and you will come to the valley and the village." She seemed to know very well that if you are twelve years old, and you are Dick Milton, the most exciting way to explore is to do it alone.

He had climbed fast, looking down, now and then, between the trees, to the village and the little river below. He had to stand still at last, because he was out of breath and because he wanted to hear the wind talking in the treetops. Just where he had stopped, an old rail fence went zig-zagging between the treetrunks, dividing somebody's land from somebody else's. It was all grown up with weeds and brambles, with long, trailing branches of blackberry bushes in its corners. He leaned on it, finding it as high as his chin, a good stout fence that might have been standing there for a hundred years. He picked a few late blackberries that shone in the sun close to his nose. They were warm and fully and sweetly ripe. The wind dropped for a minute and everything was perfectly still.

Then suddenly there was sound indeed, a crashing in the bushes, the reckless noise of wild haste, and a deer went by — a big buck, with its head thrown back and its white flag of a tail up. Dick had never before seen a deer running free, and this one was in wild flight, going in great bounds and sailing over the fence as though it had wings. Yet it stopped for a second in a little clearing just beyond, so near that the boy could see its big, frightened eyes, its golden brown sides,

dark with sweat and heaving with its spent breath.
Back in the woods there was a sharp yelp; the deer
swung and vanished in the trees, and the dog came on,
following in hot pursuit.

The dog was gold-colored too, a slim collie, his long
nose to the ground and following the line of the deer's
flight as though it had been marked in chalk. He was
yelping in high excitement; he seemed as quick as the
deer and not in the least out of breath. From far back
across the slope there came a shout, "Chris, Chris," and
the dog hesitated an instant, but then went over the
fence as lightly as a blown dandelion and disappeared
in his turn.

The owner was coming up now, making far more
noise than the dog or the deer, a tall man walking as
though one knee was a little stiff, his pleasant face
hot and worried. He called again, "Chris, Chris," and
said to Dick as he came up, "Did you see them? Which
way did they go?"

"They both jumped the fence and went up the hill,"
Dick answered.

"It's against the law to let your dog chase deer," the
man explained, anxiously. "And I saw the game
warden's truck go up the mountain road half an hour
ago. If he sees Chris he has a right to shoot him."

"I'll go after him," Dick cried quickly and was over
the fence in an instant, though certainly not with the
easy grace of the deer and the dog.

"There's a chance that they might circle back," the
man called after him. "Keep looking there above you."

Although few people know it, a persistent dog does not tire in a long race as much as a deer does, and if he can keep the deer in sight he can finally run him down. But a big buck is wise in shaking the dog off — he can make enormous leaps, breaking the trail of scent, he can turn and double. Once the dog loses sight of him, the deer will slip away silently through the bushes without breaking a twig. And most dogs, especially collies, cannot help yelping in their excitement so that the deer always knows where he is. And that was why, not many minutes later, Dick looked across the slope above him and saw a quick brown shadow go over the open space beyond a rock. The deer had turned back, and the dog, whose voice could be heard some distance on ahead, had finally turned also. The boy ran in a wild burst of breathless speed, got to the open space just as the dog reached it, and flung his arms about the collie's neck so that both went rolling over and over together on the ground.

Another dog might well have snapped, but Chris was a gentleman and a sportsman. Feeling Dick's hand firm on his collar, he gave up the chase, which he plainly knew was unlawful, got to his legs and shook himself, looking sheepish. His limp tongue hung out, long and dripping. Far away the deer had taken to full and noisy flight again and was well out of reach.

Dick found that his legs were shaky from hard running and his breath, like Chris's, was coming short. He sat down on a log, still keeping a careful hand on the dog's collar. Chris sat down beside him on the leaves and began to sniff at this stranger who had appeared so suddenly to spoil his fun. The sniffing seemed to satisfy him, for his feathery tail began to move and he leaned against the boy's knee and pushed his long nose into Dick's hand. They were sitting there together when Chris's master came tramping up the hill to sit down beside them.

Dick turned to smile at him. "He likes me," he said.

The man looked at him keenly. He had a thin face, young and sunburned, and had curly dark hair; the hand that lay on his knee was long and brown. He got a pipe out of his pocket, filled and lighted it and sat there a whole minute, silent, while Dick stroked the collie's head.

Then the man spoke. "Why shouldn't he like you?" He had the warmest and friendliest kind of smile as he asked it.

"I — I don't know," Dick replied. He looked down and moved his feet in the leaves. It was hard to say even that.

"I'm Jerry Stewart," his new acquaintance went on. "I live down there, in Jefferson Village, though I have been away for a long time, in the Navy. I just got home yesterday. So I don't place you. You're a little too old to be somebody who's been born and grown this big while I was away."

Dick said, "I'm Dick Milton." That seemed to be the way that you introduced yourself here in the New England woods to someone whose dog had started you talking together. "We haven't been here very long."

Jerry Stewart seemed to think for a moment. "Then you are grandson to Roger Devons and you live in the big house just above the town, where the mountain comes down to the road?" Dick nodded. "But," the man went on more slowly, "you don't, somehow, speak as though you were happy there."

Dick could hardly answer. He still looked down and stroked Chris behind the ears. "No," he answered, "we love the house but we aren't happy. They — they don't like us."

"And who are they?" Jerry Stewart asked sharply.

"Oh, the people all around — in the stores, in the postoffice, neighbors. They don't say anything mean or rude or anything like that, but they hardly answer when we say good morning, and none of them will work for my mother when she is trying so hard to get the house put right. Nobody had lived in it for two years and there is such a lot to do. And at the postoffice Mr. Downing just hands us out our mail without even looking at it, as though he weren't interested at all. But for all the others he studies the outside of the letters and talks about who they came from and reads all the postcards."

Jerry Stewart smiled a little, but his face was serious at once. "It's a beautiful house," he agreed. "I used to be in it often when it belonged to your grandfather. And he left it to your mother, I understand, when he died two years ago. How many of you are there?"

"There's my mother and my brother who is just

younger than me, and my two little sisters. My father is a scientist, he went for the government to South America." There was a little pause but Dick felt that he must make everything clear. "There wasn't enough money for us all to go with him, at least right away, so Mother said we would try waiting it out here in Jefferson, in the house that belongs to her. We had been stationed abroad before, and we hadn't ever been here. When we came we loved the house, but Mother saw, first, that there was something wrong about the people. It was as though they hoped we wouldn't stay. Then I saw it too."

Jerry Stewart's eyes moved across the little stretch of ground before them. "That's a ruffed grouse over there," he told Dick without letting his voice sound too loud. Dick saw a big solid bird, mottled brown and darker brown, moving about and talking to himself a little as he scratched among the leaves. Chris stirred and the bird flung himself into the air with a great burring noise of flight, and swung away, a round body with down-curving wings. Dick looked across at Jerry and smiled. Whatever might be happening down in the village, here on the windy hillside, with deer and with birds he had never seen before, things were the way he liked them. Jerry grinned back again. But Dick had a question.

"Could people—have had anything against my grand-father? But from the way Mother talks of him I am sure that couldn't be."

"Everyone loved him," Jerry answered promptly.

"Roger Devons was one of the important men of the town and every heart was warm for him. The place will never be the same without him. That is what I hear people saying everywhere, now that I have come back. If people are not treating your mother and the rest of you as they should, I don't doubt that they think they have good cause. They are very fair and square, our neighbors all about here. I have known them to make mistakes, but not in the way of being unjust. If they seem slow about getting to be friendly— and they never are very quick with strangers—certainly they are holding back for some good reason. And that is what we have to find out, what that reason is."

"We?" echoed Dick with a voice of doubt.

"We—you Miltons and me. And for a little while I am afraid it has to be mostly you. I only just got back from service overseas and now I will have to be in Washington for a while. I just stopped to get my car and to pick up Chris; a friend has been keeping him for me." Chris, hearing his name, got up and went over to settle down close to his master's knee. "I knew when people told me about your coming to the Devons house that there was something amiss there; that, somehow, they resented your having the place. I didn't think it amounted to enough to ask about it directly. And I am not sure if anyone would have told me. But if it is going to make you all unhappy, why then we have to get to the bottom of it. And the main thing is to begin."

He got out a little notebook, tore out a leaf and

wrote a name and address. "This is where you will find Mr. Andrew Styles, down near the Court House. He was your grandfather's lawyer, and my father's, too. Take your mother and go to see him. He can and will tell you at least what this is all about. He may not want to, but you can say to him that I asked him to. You may find him a little abrupt, perhaps, but he is very good at telling the truth. And inside he's all kindness."

He handed Dick the paper and got up. "Between us we are going to find this out," he finished. "We shake hands on that." He held out his long hand and Dick took it. Here was a bargain.

They walked away across the hillside, with Chris sniffing and bounding ahead. "No more deer," his master said sternly. "To heel." Chris came promptly to trot beside him, since he was a well-trained dog who only once in a while fell into wickedness.

"My mother hoped I would come across a farm somewhere; we heard there was one higher up on this hill," Dick said. "She said she wanted some eggs right off the nest."

"Why yes, that would be the Usher's place," Jerry said. "The quickest way to get there would be to go straight up through the woods until you come out on their pasture. Up above, as you will see, there is a track that leads off to their barn. Your grandfather was a good friend to them. I believe they would have eggs for you." He stood still and had a last word. "Do you think — if everything else were all right — you would like living in a little town at the foot of a mountain, up here in New England away from so many things that you are used to?"

"I know I'd like it." Dick's face lit up. The big sunny house with its sweep of view, these wide, strange woods, the fresh clean wind, all these were just what would make him happy.

"There are a good many things here in the country that will be new to you," Jerry warned. "Country living isn't as simple and peaceful as you probably think. Just be ready for anything that comes along, that is my advice. Well, good-bye. I will see you, then, as soon as I get back again."

He and Chris went on their way and Dick set his face upward. He came out on the open pasture fairly soon, and saw at some distance the rough wheel-track that slanted off toward where he caught sight of a big barn and a small house, showing over the shoulder of the hill. But just above him the ground rose steadily and beautifully, first in slippery slopes of dry grass, then in broken rocks crowned with a close group of blue-green pointed arbor vitae trees. The view must be good from up there, he thought. There was time still to go that much higher to see it.

Certainly it was well worth that last effort and the final breathless climb. He could look outward over the whole broad Champlain valley, a wide floor with little toy farms scattered over it and a white checkerboard of roads. The air was so clear that the mountains opposite, which usually looked blue, now showed ban-

ners of color across their sides. And at their feet lay
Lake Champlain, not just a bright glimpse, such as
they could see from the village, but a gleaming ribbon
of blue. And yet this was not all. For here where he
stood, the close little group of trees bordered a small
lake, too big perhaps even to be called a pond. One
end was grown up in reeds and tall grasses, but, at the
other, steep rocks went down to clear water. And as
he stood, close by a tree and not moving, there was
a whirl of wings overhead and a half dozen wild ducks
came easily down upon the surface, their wings thrust
forward to brake their speed, landing with hardly a
ripple upon the water that received them. He could
see their bright eyes, the glittering peacock green of
the feathers on their heads and necks, their neat white
collars and the gay, perfect curls of their short, shiny
tails. The water was so clear that he caught glimpses
of their orange feet, just moving a little, like the
slow blades of a propeller, keeping them aimed toward
the green weeds, which they began to pluck and gobble
with satisfied quackings. Dick could hardly tear himself
away from watching them, but the sun was high for
noon and he was a boy with a sense of time.

He turned away, the ducks rose for a minute, then
settled down again with wide rippling rings spreading
on the still water around them. He slid and ran down
the steep slope and came to the rough pasture track
which led toward the farm. There were a few cows
grazing here and there; they raised their heads question-
ingly, with that surprised look which cows always

have, and stared at him, but he was not afraid of them.
He found himself presently coming through a lane
and opposite the barn with its wide barnyard and the
gate standing open. There were chickens clucking all
about; there must be eggs. The house looked small as
compared to the barn with its sheds and corncribs
all about it, and it stood a good deal higher up the hill.
He went up toward the house door, walking slower and
slower.

"If my grandfather was friends with them, they may
not be like the people down in the village," he was
thinking. He stepped up on the big stone doorstep and
knocked.

There was a little wait, then the door opened and a
woman stood there. Yes, it was just the same, he could
see that familiar look in her face as he asked for eggs.
She only answered,

"You're the boy that lives in the Devons house,
aren't you? No, we haven't any eggs to sell you."

She was about to shut the door when a tall girl who
was washing dishes on the other side of the room turned
to speak. "I believe there must be some eggs, Mother.
I saw Sam go into the hen house to look for them.
Then Dad called him into the barn to help move the
bull into another stall. But he'll bring the eggs in
just as soon as they are through."

"Well . . ." her mother answered. She spoke reluctantly, as though she certainly did not want to sell
eggs to Dick Milton. Dick thought if she did not want
to, he had no wish to persuade her. He turned to go,

but the girl came to the door, even though he heard her mother say in a low voice:

"Don't stop him, Nora."

Nora Usher was tall, rosy, and with yellow hair — she looked about sixteen years old. Her pink cheeks grew pinker at her mother's words and she said a little awkwardly, "I'm very sorry about the eggs."

Dick only shook his head and walked away, but he was not so downhearted as he might have been, for the look Nora had given him was very friendly. He took his way again along the path toward the barn, feeling sure that the door behind him was open a little and Mrs. Usher was watching him go. And suddenly her voice rose high and shrill and frightened: "Look, look quick. The bull's got loose."

Dick looked. Between the two big open doors of the barn a great shape was moving out of the dark inside, a big heavy, black and white animal. Its huge head was dropping lower and lower and it was grumbling to itself in a deep, angry mutter of its own. A broken rope trailed down from its heavy halter. It was looking from side to side as it moved slowly out, as though making up its mind how to make the best use of this sudden bit of unexpected freedom. A voice, a boy's voice, cried out from inside the barn:

"Shut the gate. Oh, shut the gate."

At the sound the bull lifted up its head to give a great bellow that was like nothing that Dick had ever heard before, lowered its horns and came charging down at the open gate where Dick was standing.

CHAPTER TWO

Minnows for Sale

People who are eleven or twelve years old can do one thing that older ones cannot. They can notice all sorts of things, almost without knowing it, and remember them suddenly when there is need. Dick, even in the gasp that followed his first sight of the bull rushing out of the barn, had already seen, somehow, that one hinge was off the gate and knew that to shut it you would have to lift it up like the gate of the playground at his last school. He heard Nora running down from the house and saw a boy who must be Sam Usher come to the door of the barn. But there was no one near enough, no one who could be quick enough, to close the gate unless it was himself. He tugged and struggled, managed to lift the end of the gate and swung it creaking, to slam almost in the big black and white animal's face. The boy actually could feel its hot blast of breath as it set its feet and slid for a few yards in the soft ground and came to a stop. Nora Usher had come up beside him and helped him push down the stout wooden bar that held the gate in place. The bull had paused, snorted and then turned aside to snuff along the ground in search of any stray wisps of hay. A very little girl with red curls came to the fence and spoke through it. "Hi, Tommy," she said to the bull.

Most of the animals that live on farms are fully tamed and like to be where people are. The good bossies come in to be milked at the barn every night and like it, horses are proud to do the work their masters have for them, dogs are friendly and conscientious, chickens like to cluck around the feet of those that feed them. But bulls have chosen to remain wild. Somewhere deep within their unreasoning minds is a remembrance of how their great great grandfathers to a far generation used to run completely free. They do not really look on men as their enemies, but they are too big and clumsy and short-tempered to have much of that freedom allowed them. A bull does not even know what or whom he knocks over or steps on when he has a chance to rush out and claim his liberty.

Mr. Usher, a small, nimble, much sunburned man,

had come out of the barn behind his son, carrying a rope and holding a pitchfork as a threat in case the great beast charged at him. Sam Usher had run across the corner of the yard, climbed up on the fence and scrambled along the top of it, waving his arms to head the bull back to the barn. At last the big fellow, finding that he had not won freedom after all, and remembering the good feed of hay and grain in his stall inside, gave a final grunt and went lumbering away toward the big open door.

"You certainly were quick with that gate," Sam Usher said. He was a broad-shouldered boy, a little taller than Dick and evidently two or three years older. He had yellow hair like Nora's, a broad face and gay blue eyes. His sister Nora was taller still and shy. She spoke hesitatingly now.

"We surely thank you," she said. "And — and I think it was a mistake about the eggs. I will get you some out of the hen house. Betsey will help me."

She and the little red-haired girl vanished through a low doorway, and Sam, seeing the bull go lumbering into the barn with his father following cautiously, walked along beside Dick. Mrs. Usher had come down the path from the house and Dick had heard her cry out, but she was silent now and went back without a word.

"We go to the school down in the village, too," Sam Usher said to Dick. "Nora and I are in the high school building, but we saw you all go in that first day."

In these early weeks, the streams of school boys and

girls had all looked a good deal alike to Dick and he was only beginning to know some names and faces. He could not remember having caught sight of the Ushers.

Nora and Betsey came out with the eggs, big, pinkish brown ones such as one never sees in an ordinary market. "You can keep the basket," Nora said, "and bring it back when you want more." Dick paid her although she did not want to take the money and she repeated firmly, "I am quite sure we will always have some for you when you need them. You came over the top of the hill didn't you? From here it is shorter to go down by the road."

They all three walked along with him, Betsey chattering, the other two a little silent, but with the friendly silence of people who are beginning to grow acquainted. "I saw a beautiful little lake on the top of the hill," Dick told them, "and some wild ducks with blue-green on their wings coming down to the water."

"They were mallards, they're going south now," Sam observed and Betsy added eagerly:

"We go there often, we call it Our Very Own Place."

"Hush, Betsey," Nora warned. "He might like to have it for his place too."

"I would like to have it a little bit ours," Dick said. "I thought we could all come up for a picnic some day, my mother and my little sisters, they're just bigger than Betsey, and my brother Roddy. Could you come too? Would your father and mother mind?"

"No," Sam declared firmly. "I know they wouldn't mind. But it will have to be soon, for this fine October

weather won't last too long now. Do you see where that
track goes off through the gate, across the pasture? You
could take your car that way and get very nearly to
the top of the hill."

They had been going with him along the narrow,
rather rutty lane which was the Ushers' road down to
the village. They stopped now. Nora said, "We'll be
seeing you at school," and the three Ushers turned
back, Betsey looking over her shoulder for a last
smile. How good it was, Dick was thinking as he went
on down the hill, how very good to talk to people who
were ready to be friendly. He wished that he could
forget that look and those words of Mrs. Usher's.
"You're the boy living in the Devons house."

By the time he was near home he realized that he had
gone a long way indeed, and that his legs were beginning to be weary. He came up the little street that
led to their house standing big and white with
its tall round columns and the great maple trees lifting
their branches above the roof, and he felt inside, as he
always did, a thump of pleasure over thinking that
it was theirs to keep always. Most of what he remembered was apartments in busy cities, hotels in
foreign countries, staterooms on steamers. They had
moved often from one place to another, from one
country to another, because of his father's work. But
this, even already, was home.

His mother was sitting on the wide front steps,
with Dick's younger brother, Robert, who was always
called Roddy, sitting beside her. Mother always looked

pretty no matter what she was doing or what she wore. She had a blue handkerchief tied over her hair, but the curly brown ends showed just the same, and her cheeks were pink even though she looked tired. She and Roddy had been very busy ever since breakfast, up in the attic, storing away the extra boxes and suitcases they had brought. Mother had said that Dick had worked so hard all the week that he deserved some time to himself and had sent him off to explore the mountainside. There is much to do when a family settles down in a house that has been closed for some time; they had all been very busy, ever since they came.

"Have you had a good morning?" Mother asked.

For a minute Dick did not answer as he sat beside them, thinking only how pleasant it was to be comfortable and quiet in the sun, looking down at the village with its streets going downhill below them, at the clustering roofs of the houses — the wide comfortable chimneys smoking a little in the warm noon time, at the clean, high finger of the white church spire at the end of the street. Its mellow-voiced clock was striking twelve, easily and without hurry, as it had struck for a hundred and fifty years. He had to wait a little to let all this brightness and pleasure flow into him.

"It's good, isn't it?" Mother smiled at him and laid her hand on his knee.

Mrs. Towner, who lived next door to them, was walking down the street, just passing their gate. She gave them a very quick nod, and then, it seemed by

accident, turned away her head to watch a truck going by. Mother had lifted her hand to wave good morning to her, but she walked on without even glancing at the three Miltons again. Dick could see the color grow pinker in Mother's cheeks. She put her hand back on his knee. "I met a man up on the hill . . ." he began.

He told them about the deer and the dog and Jerry Stewart and how he, Dick, had been led somehow to speak of that trouble which hung over them, the fact that people in the village seemed to resent the Milton family's being there. "He told me that a friend of his could tell us what was the matter," Dick ended that part of his account. "He wrote down the name and address for me." He put his hand into his pocket to feel for the paper Jerry Stewart had given him.

Mother's face had changed as she listened, it looked suddenly worn and tired and distressed. As he felt for the paper she held up her hand. "Not now, Dick," she said. "Not — for a little while yet. I am not sure that I want to know what is the matter, until we are a little better settled, until I feel a little braver."

Dick breathed something like a sigh of relief. He had felt rather the same way. It might be something frightening and deeply disturbing, something, also, that they could not do anything about. "People look at us as though they want to be friendly and then they remember something and turn away," he said, and Mother nodded.

"We will wait a little longer," she said, "until we really feel that we live here."

Roddy spoke now, he had said nothing so far. He evidently did not like this talk of something strangely wrong between them and the people of Jefferson Village, and he turned briskly to something else. "See what I found in the attic," he said, showing Dick the square box-shaped thing which he had brought down from the attic. "Mother had seen one before, she says it is a minnow trap. You see the minnows come in here and then they can't get out, and you sell them for bait to fishermen. I'm going to put it into the brook down by the bridge and with the money I get I'm going to . . ." He stopped for he had not yet made a choice among the dozen things on which one could spend the profits of minnow-catching. "But Mother says you will have to go with me when I go down to the brook. Do you think you can after lunch, Dick? Will you? And isn't it nearly time for lunch now, Mother?"

"Yes," Mother agreed. "I was just waiting for Bella, I sent her to mail a letter. And I see her coming now." She got up and went inside to the kitchen.

Bella came in the gate, the smallest member of the Milton family, just the size to go to school for the first time this year. She had brown hair and brown eyes like Roddy's and was always quick when she moved or thought of something new. She had an even smaller girl with her. "This is Nadine," she announced. "I found her standing at her gate crying and I just said 'Come home to lunch with us,' and she came."

Mother set a place for the guest at once, but she asked a few questions since someone, surely, would be wondering where small Nadine was. The little girl was so shy that she could hardly speak, but it was finally made clear that she lived "up at the top of the road" on West Mountain back of the town, and that she spent the week days with her Aunt Cora so that she could go to school. Usually, she managed to explain, she went home for Saturday and Sunday, but this time there was no one to take her. Aunt Cora worked all of Saturday in the Bassetts Department Store, and so Nadine was left alone. "I went out to the gate, just to see some people going by, and then I couldn't — I just couldn't go back into that empty house."

Anne came in as they were sitting down, and now the set of Miltons around the table was complete. Anne was as quiet as Bella was gay and energetic. Even though she was only two years older than her small sister, she already had a way of setting about something steadily and with method, not looking at anything else until the first project was complete. She had decided to go through all the boxes and trunks in the big attic "so that someone will really know what is there and where everything is," she had begun at the stairs and was working back, so she said, to the boxes along the walls. "Some have papers," she told them, "and some have clothes but there are a few with toys." She pulled something out of her apron pocket — a little dog, made out of calico, but so well shaped and stuffed that he seemed almost ready to bark and to wag his short tail. She put it by Nadine's plate and got a shy smile, almost the first that the little girl had given anyone so far.

Roddy was impatient to get on with lunch, so that he and Dick could go down to the brook to place the precious minnow trap, and he kept urging Dick to hurry. The two boys finished before the others, having been excused by Mother, and went out carrying the clumsy wooden box between them. Dick had thought of half a dozen things which he would have liked to do with the afternoon, but he was quite willing to see, first, that Roddy got his trap moored under the bridge without falling in himself, or otherwise getting into difficulties. Roddy was ten years old and, like Bella, always eager. He could sometimes move too quickly without looking at what might lie just before him.

"What will you do for a sign?" Dick asked as they went down the road. "Somebody will have to know that you have minnows to sell."

"That's just the very thing," Roddy answered. "When Mother and I took some trash down to the dump this morning, I saw a sign lying right there on top, that said 'Minnows for Sale.' Someone had gone out of business, I expect, and thrown it away. That was what made me think of using the minnow trap to make money."

They came to the brook and the bridge that went over it, and that carried a small branch road that led away from the main one. Beyond the bridge the road climbed a long hill, at the top of which was a wide, sprawling house, with balconies and awnings and terraces for sunbaths, very different from the prim farmhouses that stood, far apart, on each side of the way.

The boys had heard that it had even a swimming pool — "though what's the use of that with the brook right here?" Roddy had said. The place belonged to a Mrs. Malvern, who came for short stays in the summer and week ends in the autumn, always with lots of visitors who rushed up and down the road in cars of every kind and color and license plates. So that people would be sure to find her, she had had a sign put up on a stout post by the bridge. It said M. Malvern, with an arrow, to guide people up the hill.

The minnow trap was a little unmanageable, but it was not long before they had got it into the water, anchored down by stones and moored by a rope to one of the supports of the bridge. They were both of them dirty and hot and not a little wet when they stood back to admire their work. "Now I have to go and get the sign," Roddy said. "The place is only just there where the road turns."

"I walk along slowly," Dick told him, quite ready now to get home and sit down with a book. "You can call after me if you need any help, and you can nail the sign to the fence anywhere — it is easy. Just don't go down to the water again by yourself." He was only pleasantly weary, but he felt that he had a right to the rest of the afternoon to himself. He sauntered slowly back toward home, and Roddy very soon joined him, pushing his hammer into a back pocket.

"I found it all right," Roddy said. "I was so afraid someone else might have taken it. And it was just right, it said 'Minnows for Sale,' and there was only one little corner split off. I wrote my name in crayon in the corner, though there wasn't much room. I found a good solid place to nail it. Now I wonder how soon anyone will see it."

"You'd better say how soon will the minnows see it," Dick said. But Roddy had peered over the edge of the bridge and had seen little fish already gathered curiously around it and quite ready to go inside.

When they came home the house was very quiet. The three girls were upstairs in Anne's room, and Mother seemed to be taking a nap. Roddy went down to the cellar on some business of his own and Dick went to his own room — it was the first he had ever had all to himself — took a book from the box that was not yet quite unpacked, and lay down on the couch opposite the window. Mother had piled it with plump gay pillows, against which he settled comfortably. He opened the book, but almost at once he dropped off to sleep.

He was awakened by voices downstairs and sat up suddenly. They were loud voices — no, it was only one — a woman's, and it sounded very shrill and angry. What in the world could it mean? He jumped up and ran downstairs, still blinking. He could hear Mother in Anne's room, talking to the little girl Nadine. It seemed that Nadine was crying.

A big car had driven up to the door, with a chauffeur in a black cap at the wheel; there was only one such car and driver — and owner, in the town. It was that same Mrs. Malvern who lived in the great house over beyond

the river and the bridge. She must have just come to
spend the week end, for there were suitcases and dressing bags piled on the front seat. She was leaning over
the car door and talking very loud, not to anybody in
particular, but plainly intending to be heard all
through the house. Roddy was the only one who had
come out when the car drove up; he stood now on the
top step, astonished and unspeaking, while the stream
of words washed over him.

"Perfectly outrageous," Mrs. Malvern was saying;
she was almost shouting. "I never heard of such im-
pudence . . . They said in the village it was one of the
boys from this house . . . I demand to see your mother
at once."

Mrs. Milton had come down now and was standing
beside Roddy, with her hand on his shoulder. "I don't
quite understand what this is all about," she said
quietly when Mrs. Malvern had at last stopped for
want of breath.

"Then just come with me and see for yourself," the
angry lady responded. "Get in the car, the two boys
can sit in front with Phillips. I know they had something to do with it. Just come and see."

"I am very sorry, I cannot come," Mother said. "I
cannot leave my two little girls alone and there is
something wrong with their small guest. She is crying
dreadfully. But the boys will go with you."

They did not go willingly but they went. Phillips,
the chauffeur, stopped the car just by the bridge
and Mrs. Malvern pointed. Then they saw. Roddy had

not looked about very much and had chosen the first good strong post for his sign, and there it stood. At the top the name M. Malvern and below it the straggling dirty announcement, "Minnows for Sale." It did look a little, a very little, as though it was Mrs. Malvern who was setting up in the minnow business and not Roddy Milton. His little scrawl of a name in the corner was not very easy to see.

Both the boys were out of the car in an instant and Phillips was behind them. Dick thought he could see the corner of the man's mouth twitching, but there was nothing else. Roddy had nailed the sign so tightly that the chauffeur had to get a hammer and pliers out of the trunk to get it off. It split while he was at work on it and Phillips handed the pieces gravely to Roddy, who took them and threw them into the brook. Then Roddy walked down to the edge of the water, pulled in the minnow trap, opened the wooden gate and let all the little fish swim away free. "There were a lot of them in it," was all that he said.

Dick spoke up. "We are dreadfully sorry. It was my fault as much as his. I didn't wait to watch him put up the sign. He's only ten years old and he didn't think of how it looked. We'll come tomorrow and fill up the nail holes with putty. And I think hardly anybody but you could have seen it."

Mrs. Malvern was not to be satisfied. "Perfectly outrageous," she kept repeating. She had a last word. "You live in the Devons house, I see. Well, one good thing is that, from all I hear, you won't be there long."

Phillips started the car. He touched his cap to the boys as he drove away.

The two boys burst into the house, scarcely able to wait to tell their mother what had happened. But she was at the telephone and could not speak to them at that moment. She was talking to Nadine's Aunt Cora who, it seemed, was Mrs. Markley, and who had a telephone voice which filled the entire hall.

"The child's been crying, you say?" Mrs. Markley was asking. "Now I can't think what for."

Mother glanced up the stairs but the door of Anne's room was closed and Nadine could not hear. "Nadine is perishing with homesickness," she answered firmly. "She's little and she's away from home for the first time. We will be glad to take her home, my children and I, and if necessary go and get her on Sunday evening so that she can go to school again on Monday morning. That is, if you are willing."

Mrs. Markley seemed to hesitate. "I don't like her to be beholden to strangers," she returned, not very graciously. "I don't know as I would have said she could come and eat at your house if I had been there. But then I just hardly know what to do about the child. I guess I'd just as soon you took her home if you really want to. I'll look for her Sunday evening."

Nadine's lingering sobs, which had begun at the moment when she thought she must go back again to her aunt's empty house, stopped by magic now, when she was told that she was going home. They all climbed hastily into the old rattly station wagon; Miltons were

always ready to go on an expedition and the faithful
station wagon always seemed able and willing to do its
share. With Nadine telling them how to go, they set off
up the steep rough road which led away from the
village in a direction they had not yet gone. It ran between stony fields at first, then through woods, then
passed a clearing where a bare, shabby house which had
never seen a coat of paint stood near a rushing mountain stream. A boy was splitting wood in the untidy
yard; he looked up and nodded to Dick.

"That's Rob Dale," Dick told his mother. "He's in
my class at school. Everyone says he's awfully smart."
It was something of a shock to see that he lived in such
a poor, unlovely house, even more of a shock to hear
a woman's shrill voice call out from inside:

"Rob, ain't you never goin' to finish with that wood
and feed the calves?"

They crossed the little bridge above the brook, with
its boards rattling loose under the wheels of the car.
They climbed up and up, turning, as Nadine told them,
in this direction and that as roads branched off to
lonely farms scattered across the mountainside. At last
they came to the gate of her house, a small house and
white and low, with big wind-tossed trees around it,
and bright flowers still blooming beside the door. They
let Nadine out and waited only to see her being happily
received by two pretty older sisters at the door, then
waved good-bye and set off homeward. It was getting
late and there would not be much more daylight. "I
should hate to drive on this road when it is really

dark," Mrs. Milton said. It was on the way down, after they had left Nadine, that the two boys told their mother about Mrs. Malvern and what she had said.

"I can't think what she meant," Roddy said over and over, "about our not being here long."

"We'll probably find out about it now," Dick answered, but he still had the feeling that he did not want to know too soon. There were pleasanter things to think about.

On Monday, when he was at school again, Dick noticed Rob Dale more particularly as he came in. For the first time, Dick saw how shabby this other boy's clothes were, how his shock of light brown hair needed cutting, and how he had outgrown the length of his coat sleeves and his trousers. There was mud on his shoes as though he had walked far — through wet woods, perhaps — for Nadine had said that there was a short path down the mountain from where Rob lived. Well, there were far worse things than going down a mountain path early in the morning on a bright October day. Rob Dale gave him a rather surly nod, almost as though he hated to think that Dick had seen how mean and poor a house he lived in. But he took his seat without saying anything. It was quite plain, as the classes went through their work of the day, that Rob Dale's thin, clever face stood indeed for a quick and able mind.

It was a few days later that Dick and Sam Usher had arranged to meet after school so that Sam could come home with him and show him how to put up some shelves for his mother in the kitchen. Dick, al-though he liked books and birds and animals better, still was good at tools, but Sam was better. Sam was going to stop for Dick when he finished an experiment in the high school laboratory. "I'll wait for you in the library, off the big assembly room," Dick told him.

The other pupils trooped out while Dick sat reading, but he could hear a group of teachers talking to his own teacher, Miss Evans, at her desk, which was near the library door.

"Yes, he gave me the wrist watch for my birthday — look how nicely it is engraved on the back," Miss Evans was saying. She was going to be married and there was much laughing and joking about her plans and this gift from her fiancé. But now the bell rang for the teachers' meeting and they all hurried away, just as she took it off to show the others.

Dick finished the chapter he was reading and put the book on the shelf. Sam must be coming, for he heard footsteps in the schoolroom outside. He stepped to the library door, and noticed that Miss Evans, in her hurry, had left her watch on the desk. He drew a quick breath when he saw that it was not Sam but the big boy Rob Dale who had come in, who had stepped up on the teachers' platform and stood staring down at the watch.

If he had only had time to collect his wits, Dick would have drawn back, but he had already taken a step into the schoolroom and Rob Dale had seen him. The two stared at each other for a long moment, neither knowing what to say. Rob Dale burst out first.

"Yes, I know what you're thinking, you believe that I'd steal it, don't you? Go ahead and tell the teacher and see what she says. But who would believe you? Don't you know the talk that's going on about you here in the village, about your living in that house, all of you, when you haven't any right to? You just ought to know what people are saying!"

A voice spoke suddenly at the door. "That will be enough of that, Rob Dale."

Sam Usher had come in to look for Dick. The Dale boy gave Sam a strange look, stepped down off the platform and strode away to the door without another word. Sam tried to smile at Dick, but the boy was white-faced as he asked —

"You heard what he said? What did he mean?"

Sam only shook his head. "Somebody else will have to tell you," he said miserably. "I can't do it."

CHAPTER THREE

Rain on Saturday

Dick and Sam Usher walked slowly along the street toward Dick's house, neither having a word to say to the other. A little ahead of them Dick's sister Bella was walking home with little Nadine; the two were chattering away both at once, with bursts of laughter at intervals. Bella, at least, had made a friend, and Nadine most surely was quite happy again.

They had gone, the Milton family, up West Mountain again late on Sunday afternoon to bring Nadine back to the village in time for Monday morning school, as they had promised. The road was as steep and lonely as it had seemed to them the first time, and, as they passed it, Rob Dale's house seemed more forlorn and dilapidated even than before. As they climbed higher and higher, Anne had said, "These hills look so cold, Mother." It was quite true. There was here none of the smiling greenness that showed on the slopes above the Champlain valley and the view over which their own house looked out.

Nadine's house, however, was as cheery and cosy inside as one could desire, her two tall older sisters bade them a warm welcome, and Mrs. Wilmer, Nadine's mother, a small woman with smooth dark hair, came in to greet them with the most earnest and happy thanks for their having understood how homesick the little girl was and how she needed exactly that break in her stay in the village.

"She's quite cheerful and happy about going back to school now," Mrs. Wilmer said. "It is hard for her, I know, staying there with her aunt, who never had any children and doesn't understand them very well. But she was willing to take her in, and Nadine was as anxious as any of us that she should go to school. Her sisters are so much older they had finished before it was time for Nadine to begin. Can I give you a cup of tea, Mrs. Milton?"

"Everyone knows who we are," Dick had thought a little bitterly, "but no one wants to know any more."

"My other sister would have taken her," Mrs. Wilmer had gone on, pouring out milk for Dick and Roddy and Anne and Bella. "She is so kind and motherly and has such a pleasant household with her husband and her three children. But she lives up on the hill above Jefferson and it is a mile and a half that the children have to go down to the school, since the bus doesn't go up there. But I would have liked Nadine to be with her. She is Mrs. Usher."

Dick had turned his head to stare, for certainly these were not words that he would have used to describe Mrs. Usher. He remembered himself in time to turn away, but he kept going over in his mind what Nadine's mother had said. Kind? He would never have called Mrs. Usher that. But he had only seen her once!

He asked Sam now, as they went on together, saying nothing since they had left the school. "Is it true that Nadine's mother is your aunt?"

"Why yes," answered Sam, evidently glad to have something they could talk about at last. "We would all have liked to have Nadine stay with us, instead of with Aunt Cora in the village, but we knew she could never make that long walk every day. Betsey is too little for school, so it doesn't matter yet."

Sam seemed to think that he, too, must find something to say and he asked, "About those shelves? Did your mother just want something for now, or were they to be built so that they would stay always?"

"To stay there always." Dick's answer sounded fierce in its earnestness, but Sam went on easily to talk of how deep and wide they ought to be, a question which they were discussing as they turned in at the gate. They went at once down to the workshop in the basement

and were soon so busy that there was no need of further
talk between them, and the bitter memory of those
words spoken an hour ago began to slip away. Sam was
invited to stay for supper, but he went home immediately after to help with the evening chores.

He said as he was leaving, "We talked about a picnic
a while ago. We will have to have it soon for this good
weather will not hold much longer." It was arranged
at once that it would be next Saturday.

Mrs. Milton seemed greatly pleased with the idea
and the two little girls were radiant. They had not yet
been up the mountain behind the house, and were full
of curiosity about the little lake, the wide view, the
Ushers and their farm. Bella wanted to see Betsey, "Because I want to have a friend that I'm the oldest of."
Small and mouselike as Nadine Wilmer was, she still
was six months older than Bella. Mother was already
planning about fried chicken and how many sandwiches. Dick stood on the porch under the big columns,
watching Sam walk away toward home. Inside there
were gay voices and much laughter, his mother's the
gayest of all. Could he go in and tell her of the thing
that Rob Dale had said to him that day: "Don't you
know what the people in the village are saying about
you?" The words went marching through his mind
again and again, along with his own question to Sam:
"What did he mean?" That Sam could not answer him
was the worst thought of all.

He'd wait to tell Mother until after the picnic, he
made up his mind. He knew that his mother thought

well of Sam Usher, and that she was happy that he had at least one friend. Yet perhaps in the end he would find that even Sam was no friend of his. He would go on thinking that Sam was, as long as it was possible.

On the next day it rained, the wind blew high and loud and it seemed that for people who were planning picnics, all was lost. But the weather cleared again, and, though the leaves had come down in a storm of fluttering color and the trees were bare now, the air was warm and hazy and made any person who was inside of four walls long to be out of doors. Dick sat in school, at his desk near the window, and watched the towering white clouds roll across the sky. He saw a flock of quail go clucking and bustling along the school fence, while the big cock bird of the party flew up to the highest bar and whistled his rich "Bob-white, bob-white," to call his little group together. He glanced up and saw the teacher looking at him, but she only smiled. Perhaps she knew that he was a boy who was not used to a schoolroom where you could see quail and clouds and far rolling hills. Perhaps she was only just happy and not thinking about him at all.

Saturday came with perfect weather; no one could have asked for anything better. This would surely be the last picnic of the year, and everything must be perfect to match the day. They were all of them busy through the whole morning, finishing and packing the sandwiches, wrapping up the chicken and the hard-boiled eggs, polishing the apples, and trying to remember things like salt and sugar and extra spoons. Roddy helped Dick carry the baskets and blankets out to the car and they all scrambled in.

They had to go slowly up the narrow rutted lane and, under Dick's direction, turned carefully at the lower edge of the Usher farm into the rough track across the pasture. There was room to skirt the big stones safely and they mounted up and up until they were very close to the little lake. They stopped the car beyond the trees, made their fire between two big rocks and raked out the coals to roast their potatoes and heat the chicken. The Ushers came, presently, by the short way up from their house, carrying a basket which held a deep, rich, and wonderfully fragrant apple pie.

There was much noise and laughter and everybody gave directions to everybody else and nobody paid much attention. Sam showed himself to be a remarkable hand with a fire and Nora showed the finest skill in making cocoa. There was sudden quiet when Mother said grace and eight hungry people began to eat. They were already well acquainted, all of them. Betsey and Bella had struck up just the friendship which Bella had hoped for; Anne and Nora, in spite of the difference in their ages, had taken to each other at once. Sam Usher sat between Roddy and Dick, the three of them full of talk of boys' affairs.

They were full and sleepy and lazy when they finished, and willing — even Roddy and Betsey and Bella — to sit quietly and look out at the broad valley where the hayfields had been cut on the farms, and everything was brown and yellow, with the blue wall

of mountains beyond. A little wind was blowing across the hilltop, rippling the lake and rustling the trees beyond which the station wagon stood. A little fox, a very small and inexperienced one, stole out alongside of a sheltering rock and dropped his sleek, red-gold head to the water for a wary drink. The wind was behind him so that he did not get a sniff of the human creatures so near to him, but he seemed very uneasy, as though he knew that there was something unusual today about what was plainly his Very Own Place too. He slipped away when a rolling pebble startled him, and though they sat watching and keeping perfectly still, he did not come back. Then Sam held up his hand and said softly, "Hark." Far away there was that faint, wild honking that everyone knows, the voices of flying geese.

They could see, dark against a cloud, the two long lines meeting at a point, a great flock of geese that came swiftly nearer and nearer. And then suddenly those smooth dark flying shapes with outstretched necks paused, circled, and then came dropping down out of the sky in a thunder of wings and a tumult of gabbling voices. They covered the whole of the little lake and the shore, they strutted along with heads up and white breasts out, with their big, black-marked bills turning from side to side. It was a sight like nothing else, these bold confident creatures, plunging in to swim a little, coming out to shake the water off their feathers, to jostle each other and walk about in the sun and talk.

It was that moment which was chosen by the little fox to come back and finish his drink. He did not seem to be afraid of the big birds. Perhaps it was a well-known saying in the fox family that a full-grown fox — if he is lucky and only then — can master a full-grown Canada goose. At least he came trotting easily down to the edge of the shore and was quite unprepared when three big birds rushed at him, knocked him over with a blow of a long wing, hissed and shouted at him, and, when he got to his feet, dazed and bewildered, struck at him again.

The party under the trees all cried out, but the geese were making such a noise that people's voices could scarcely be heard. Betsey was nearest to the edge of the water and she was the one to take action.

"You bad birds," she cried out at them and ran down to the shore, flapping her apron and shouting "Shoo." The geese were not afraid of a little fox, but human beings are such dangerous enemies that they were thoroughly and foolishly afraid of even this small one. With a tremendous honking and beating of wings they all took off, mounting upward, circling until the whole flock was in the air and then stretching their necks and winging away in their long lovely arrow. Soon they were once again only a mark in the sky.

"Well done, Betsey," Mother said as the little girl came back to them, smoothing her apron and looking pleased that the little fox had got safely away.

And now it would soon be dark, for autumn afternoons are short and they must set about packing things up again to go home. "I thought we would have finished a little earlier," Mother said to Nora Usher. "I had wanted to go down to your house and meet your mother, even if only for a moment. But it has got too late now." Dick, standing beside his mother, thought that Nora Usher looked startled, even a little frightened at Mrs. Milton's proposal, and relieved at her last words.

"Some time you must," she said politely but the invitation came with a good deal of hesitation. Dick thought of Nadine's mother and the words she had used to describe her sister, Mrs. Usher.

"No," he said to himself fiercely, remembering her cold look and her answer when he came to her door that first day. Never, he was sure, could he use the word *kind* in thinking or talking of Mrs. Usher. And now the loading was finished and the three Ushers stood to watch them go, as the station wagon threaded its way along the narrow crooked track, its lights stabbing far into the dark as the Miltons took their way homeward.

Sam Usher had been right about the change in the weather, for by another Saturday everything was different. Every last leaf was gone from the trees, and, as Dick woke in the morning he could hear the cold rain splashing against the windows and the loud wind sweeping through the big maple branches above the roof. At breakfast there was much discussion of plans for the day, since everything had to be rearranged on account of the weather.

"Perhaps you would begin looking through the boxes

of papers in the attic, Dick," Mother said. "I need to know which have letters, which have accounts and bank reports and such things. It will help us both a great deal, when we go through them together later, to know beforehand which are the ones with the most important things for us to look at."

Dick had thought that today there might be a quiet hour in which he could tell his mother of that afternoon when Rob Dale had spoken so roughly to him, had used those hard words, "Living in that house that you have no right to." He had put it off and put it off, but surely he must tell her soon. Yet today, when she was so busy, still did not seem to be the right time. She was settling the kitchen cupboards, now that the painting was done and the new shelves were up. Dick, as he turned to go upstairs, saw Anne scampering ahead of him. She, too, seemed to have decided that this rainy day was good for attics.

She had given only the briefest glance to the rows of chests with papers and to the filing cases on the shelves; those were for Dick and Mother to go through later. It was Dick's task now to see which held family letters and which only bundles of old checks, bills and receipts. He squatted down before the first one and raised the lid; Anne went to her own corner and began lifting out the rolls of silk and the little bundles of velvet and lace which gather in everyone's attic on the distant chance that they will be used again some day, but whose existence has generally been forgotten by the time that possible day arrives. The rain was very loud on the roof so close above their heads. It was pleasant to feel sheltered and cosy inside, with both of them knowing that they were in good, though silent, company.

Presently, much to the surprise of both of them, there was other company. Feet, unfamiliar feet, came slowly up the attic stairs, and a woman appeared — broad, cheery-faced and full of energy, carrying a big basket full of wet and steaming clothes.

"You don't know me," she observed, as she came between the rows of boxes and set her basket down, "but I'm Martha Jenkins and I live over at the other edge of town and I come once a week, Saturdays, to wash for Mamie Towner that lives next to you. I expect you know her by now?" She paused, for this was a question, and Dick made a small noise that might be taken for an answer of any kind, and her talk went flowing on. "It was always fixed that when it rained I could bring the wash over here and hang it in Mr. Devons' attic to dry, since there's no proper space in Mamie's house, not room enough to swing a cat in. Mr. Devons — he was your grandfather, wasn't he? — always said to come right along, no matter whether he was at home or not, and I still came even after he was gone and the house was closed. So today, Mamie was out when I came, but I thought I'd just ask if it was all right to do the same thing, and your mother down in the kitchen — and a sweet lady she is, I saw that in a minute — she said to go right on up."

She had got down a clothesline from its place on a

shelf, and Dick went to help her string it across the open space where the wet clothes could hang. He did not care much about being interrupted, but Anne, it seemed, could talk, or rather listen, and go through boxes at the same time, so that she and Mrs. Jenkins were soon deep in conversation and he could put his mind once more on what he was doing. Most of the letters which he unfolded were brief and of the same kind: "We thank you for your very generous contribution" — to the Camp for Crippled Children, or the 4-H Club or the Scholarship fund of the nearby State University. One, badly written, was almost as short, but was a little different. "Herewith I am returning the money you lent me three years ago, you may know that I could not rest until I could pay it back. The chance it gave me has done like you said, it has made a man of me. All I needed was to get out of Jefferson where I had made such a bad start, and I want you to know that now I am living different than I did before. I have steady work and am keeping it, the way you said you wanted to hear about. You have my thanks and I will never forget you. Hoping you are in good health —" The name at the end meant nothing to Dick but he smiled over what it told him about his grandfather. "I expect he thought no one but those two would ever know," he said to himself.

There was a thick bundle of papers next and as he took time to untie them, he caught some of the talk that was going on, not exactly between Anne and Mrs. Jenkins, because Mrs. Jenkins was doing most of it.

Anne had brought out a patchwork quilt and was holding it up. Even Dick could see that the little flowered blocks and the intricate pattern made it an unusually beautiful one.

"Yes, and look there, it's all finished but that last quarter of it, down in the corner. I've seen it before, when I was a little girl, and heard the story to it. Miss Isabel Mead, a sweet pretty girl she was, they tell me, when she was young — I only saw her after she was gray-haired — it was she that made it. She was going out one evening with her young man that she was promised to and she made herself a new dress for the party, all flounces it was and drapery on the front of the skirt, made it out of this flowered stuff. They went off together so happily, but somehow they had a little tiff before the evening was over, and when he brought her home she wouldn't say good night to him. Going to be married they were in not many weeks. The next day she waited from morning to evening for him to come and say he was sorry, so they could make it up, but he didn't come and she went on waiting. It had really been her fault, but she was high-spirited and she wasn't going to admit it. So she still went on waiting, but he had his spirit too, so he didn't come. At last she sent word through someone else that if he didn't want to come he needn't, and so when the time came there wasn't any wedding."

Anne was listening with all her ears, and even Dick had stopped pretending that he was untying a packet of papers and had put them back into the chest.

"And a year went by and then another," Mrs. Jenkins proceeded, still busy with sorting out and hanging up the clothes. "Miss Isabel ripped up the new dress, made for the party, for she knew she would never wear it again. She set out to make it into a quilt and she sewed away on it, week after week. And then one day, while she was sitting in her room at work on it — " Mrs. Jenkins' mouth was full of clothespins, but she went on just the same, — "all at once the gate opened and *he* was coming in. She dropped her sewing and flew to open the door and each of them said the same thing at the same minute. 'I'm sorry. I love you.' "

"And so they were married after all?" Anne said as Mrs. Jenkins paused at last.

"Yes dear, they were married and the young man's name was Devons and in good time he got to be your great grandfather. And she never put another stitch into the quilt but you see she kept it always. There now, that's just another story that an old woman will tell young things about their elders. But seeing the quilt right there brought it all back as though it were the first day I heard it myself."

Anne got up to shake it out so that she could see the whole pattern. Dick came across to help her and together they hung it in a spare space on the clothesline. Even though the attic was dark on that rainy morning they could see that it was a thing of real beauty, its colors still rosy and green and glowing, its pattern perfect — as far as it went.

"Why, it's almost finished," Anne said, "and see, here

are all the last patches, cut up and rolled together. I believe I could finish it for a Christmas present for Mother. Do you think I could? Would you help me?"

"I'll help you indeed," the good woman said. "With all my heart."

"She says she lives out at the edge of town," Dick was thinking. "So maybe she doesn't know what people are saying about us — whatever it is that they are saying." The sharp memory had come back with a stab.

But if Mrs. Jenkins did not know, she was not to go much longer in ignorance. Someone was coming up the stairs in a hurry, breathing hard. Mrs. Towner, their neighbor, stood at the door, a thin woman, full of angles and out of breath from climbing stairs and for other reasons.

"Martha Jenkins," she said, "what do you mean by bringing the wash over here without asking anyone?"

"I asked the lady of the house, and a proper lady she is," Martha returned stoutly. "And you wasn't in and you didn't say anything beforehand. How was I to know what to do?"

"You know what to do now," was the tart answer.

"Take those things down and carry them back home. I don't want to be beholden to people I don't know."

"They're your neighbors, Mamie," Mrs. Jenkins said.

"I don't know them," Mamie Towner repeated.

Martha Jenkins pursed her lips, hesitated, then began removing clothespins and taking down the heavy clammy sheets, the ruffled pillow cases, the gathered petticoats which seemed highly in fashion, but had really held over their gathers and flounces from a much earlier day. No one said a word as the clothes came down. Anne, and then Dick came to help her and get the miserable minutes over, while Mamie Towner stood, stiff and immovable at the door.

"We'll take the basket down," Dick said, for the wet clothes were heavy. He and Mrs. Jenkins carried it between them, down the long stairs, across the lawn in the pouring rain, to Mrs. Towner's back door. Anne walked beside Dick and the owner of the clothes followed after. Mrs. Jenkins lifted the basket over the threshold and spoke very briefly. "People hadn't ought to make fools of themselves about nothing," she said. The two Miltons withdrew, Mrs. Towner came in out of the rain and the door closed with a slam.

Mrs. Milton was stirring something in a pot that smelled very good as they came into the kitchen. "Oh, yes, Mrs. Towner did speak to me when she came in, but only to say that she wanted to go upstairs. I knew in a minute what she would say when she got there." Mother sat down in the big kitchen rocking chair, took Anne on her lap and began to laugh as she had evidently been wanting to do ever since her first sight of Mamie Towner's face. Roddy came pounding up from the shop in the basement.

"What's all this?" he demanded. "I could hear you girls giggling all the way down there." The others had to tell him. Somehow after the first few minutes, Dick could not go on thinking that it was very funny.

It was not until after supper that he had a chance to take Mother aside in the big quiet parlor, and put the whole thing together, Mrs. Malvern's sharp words to Roddy, Rob Dale's lashing out at Dick as being no better than himself even though he was, apparently, just about to steal Miss Evans' watch, now Mrs. Towner who was so determined to accept no favors from "people she didn't know." "Though I think she has had to work pretty hard not to know us," Dick finished.

Mother was very prompt in coming to a conclusion. "Where is that paper you had in your pocket that this Mr. Jerry Stewart gave you?" she said. "We should have taken his advice at once, we have put off hearing something disagreeable much too long." She went into the hall, took down the telephone receiver, and made swift arrangements. "Mr. Styles is in his office this evening and he will see us," she told Dick. "We will go now. I shall need you to go with me."

They settled with the others that the dishes should be left to be washed when they came home. "Dick and I have an errand," was all Mother explained. She went upstairs to get ready and so did Dick. When they came down she looked very smart in her black suit with white ruffles showing. Dick had on his corduroy jacket and his hair brushed down smoothly, the way it was when people called him Richard. They went out together. What they were going to learn might be—anything. It might be frightening, it might be very hard to hear. But now they would really know.

CHAPTER FOUR

A White Christmas

When they came in, Dick's first thought was that Mr. Andrew Styles' office had a great deal of paper in it, spread out on desk and tables, and that the walls were made entirely of books, fat brown ones all looking exactly alike. Mr. Styles himself did not look like anybody else at all, he was long and bony and had a thin face with hollows and shadows on it from the light beside him. It was a gentle face but a very serious one, and he did not smile when he got up to greet them and to say, "Yes, Mrs. Milton, of course I know all about you. I have had various matters of business to talk over with you, but have been waiting to bring them up until you were a little more settled."

Mother sat down and Dick perched on a high stool beside her. "Even though my father lived here a number of years, I was not in Jefferson often," she said. "It was not until after my mother died and after I was married that he came here, bought back his father's house and settled down to live where he had lived when he was a boy. And my husband and my children and I have always been so very far away, that the children have never been in Jefferson at all. Only Dick ever saw my father, and that was not to remember him. I wish he could have known his grandfather better." Mr. Styles seemed to be waiting for them to explain why they had come to see him, so Mother added, "A Mr. Jerry Stewart suggested to Dick that we should come to ask you something. Dick will tell you."

"Yes?" was all that Mr. Styles said, turning his eyes to Dick.

Dick told him. "People are — as though nobody wanted to be friends with us," he explained, "without ever trying to find out what we are really like." He added a little more but there was really not so very much to say. Mr. Styles asked a quiet question or two. "Were people really rude?" he wanted to know. "Not everybody, only just some. And some people almost look at us as though they wanted to be friends, and then they seem to think of something and turn their heads away."

Mr. Styles was silent for a minute. "Perhaps he isn't

going to be willing to tell us," Dick thought in panic, and he fell back on his one real friend whom he had met in the woods. "Mr. Jerry Stewart, that I saw up on the mountain, wanted me to say to you that he would like you to tell us what is the matter."

"I have been wanting to tell you myself," Andrew Styles answered. "You have the right to know. The reason for all this is very simple, but the remedy — that is another thing." Dick and Mother leaned forward and waited and at last the statement came. "People here in Jefferson do not approve of your coming to live in the Devons house. They believe you have no right to. And I will tell you why. Four years ago a younger friend of your grandfather's gave over to him a sum of money, quite a large amount as we here in Jefferson look at it, and asked Roger Devons to take charge of it and invest it for him, since he himself was to be away for a good stretch of time. You know what investing is?" He broke off to ask Dick. The boy nodded.

"It means buying stocks and bonds and things," he ventured and Mr. Styles seemed to think that was enough. "When the friend came back, your grandfather had died and there was no sign or record of his money, or any word of what Roger Devons had done with it. The friend is not a very business-like fellow, he cannot remember whether your grandfather ever gave him a receipt for the money, and says if he did he has lost it, in Korea or Japan or Formosa or some other of the many places where he has been. Therefore there is nothing to show that he has a claim on any part of your grandfather's estate."

Mother's hands were clasped very tight in her lap, Dick knew that she was trying not to speak hastily, but to let Mr. Andrew Styles go on to make this strange matter clear.

"In a village like this," Andrew Styles went on, "everybody knows all about everybody else. These people are very kind and they are also very just. They have made up their minds, amongst themselves, that Roger Devons, who was the soul of honesty, might perhaps have lost the money by a mistaken investment, or lost a good part of it. They would not blame him for that; every man makes mistakes. Your grandfather did not leave any great sum when he died, and they believe that, if he had lost his friend's money, he should have left the house to him. It is worth just about the amount which cannot be accounted for. That is all. They believe it is not rightful that you should be living in that house. Whenever they see you they think about it; they are waiting to be friends until the whole matter is put right." Mr. Styles' whole manner changed suddenly. "Do you like the house?" he asked.

"We love it," Dick answered at once. "It feels like home, more than any place we have ever lived before. We've done a lot of scrubbing and painting and clearing up the garden — Mother the most, of course, but we've all helped. When you work so hard on something it seems to be more yours than by any other way."

"I agree with you," the lawyer said. "And it may be that just by seeing you work so hard over it, these village neighbors will come to think — to understand — that the place is yours and ought to be."

"But if it isn't ours," Mother said quickly. "If it really should belong to someone else, what are we to do? Who is this friend who ought to have it?"

"Not quite so fast," Mr. Styles said, holding up his hand. "I cannot tell you the name of the friend without being given express permission. There is no doubt in the world that the place is yours, fully and truly by law, for your father owned it and left it to you, Mrs. Milton." He got up, searched for a little in a row of pigeon holes and came back with a square paper which he unfolded. "I am not sure that you know just how much land goes with the house; there is a good deal more than you probably have been told. It is mostly rough mountain land and not worth very much except that the Usher farm is part of the property. The Ushers are your tenants, Mrs. Milton, did you know that?"

"Oh dear, are they?" Mother exclaimed so anxiously that Andrew Styles smiled at last.

"Yes, it cannot be denied," he said. "And also it cannot be denied that they have not been able to pay their rent for four months or more. Things have been hard with them. A shed burned down in the spring and they lost a cow or two. Fortunately they do own a rather valuable bull; I feel sure Roger Devons helped them buy it."

"The bull's name is Tommy," Dick said, though it did not seem very important.

"I have been acting in a way as agent for your father's affairs," Mr. Styles went on, "and have kept the taxes paid and such things. But I have not taken any steps about the unpaid rent."

"What do I have to do about it?" Mother asked, her voice more and more disturbed. Mr. Styles laughed out loud, a very kind and happy sort of laugh.

"You will have to decide that," he insisted. "But the Ushers are good honest people and your father was very fond of them. I do not believe you are going to be hard on them."

He unfolded the paper fully to show that it was a map of the hillside, and outlined the Usher's farm at the very top. "Here is how your land runs," he pointed with a pencil, "back uphill from the house quite a distance as you see. Here are the woods, here is the fence that divides your property from Mrs. Towner's, who is your neighbor. And now here above is the pasture and the cleared fields, with the Usher's barns over here, and their house."

"Is the pond ours?" Dick began to ask, but did not get beyond the first word. The pond belonged to the Usher children, it was their Own Place. He had no right to push that question. Mr. Styles was folding up the map. "I will give this to you," he said. "I was waiting for a proper chance. And now, since we are beginning to feel a little acquainted, tell me about some of these people and what they have said and done to disturb you so." Dick found that he could tell him easily, about Mrs. Towner and the washing, about Mrs. Malvern and the minnows, about Rob Dale. Mr. Styles smiled over Mrs. Towner, and laughed thoroughly over Mrs. Malvern. "Maria has a sharp tongue, that is true, and she always says what is in her thoughts at that minute. But her thoughts change very rapidly. He looked grave over what had burst from Rob Dale. "He said you ought to know what people are saying about you? Now you do know. So we go forward from there."

Mother got up. It was time to go and they had got the answer to their question. Her face showed that she was not yet satisfied, indeed she was very far from it. "But if the place really ought not to be ours . . ." she said again.

"If Roger Devons did something wrong with his friend's money, and lost it without making any effort at return, then you might come to feel that the house was not really yours. But I am as certain as I am of anything in this world that he did not. And it is not only because Jerry Stewart sent you to me that I trust you to do what is right. Now that you are here, now that you can go through your father's papers, Mrs. Milton, now that every one of you can keep his and her eyes and ears open, you are bound to find the real truth some time. Somewhere, there is somebody who knows and can tell you what has really happened. And the day when you can come to me and say that you know in full what is the real answer to this question, that will be one of the happiest days of my life." He came down the little flight of stairs with them and stood at the outer door. He looked from Dick's earnest face to the troubled one of his pretty mother.

"People are standing off from you, but it is not from unkindness. If you were in any sort of real difficulty, they would find their way to you and ask if they could help you. And I believe," he smiled down on Dick, "that you will find them breaking down, one by one, for I do not think they can stand long against you. You say Martha Jenkins is on your side already. Well, there will be more."

The rain had stopped entirely as they walked home and the air and the stars had a clear sparkle. They stepped along briskly and laughed together, for the visit to Mr. Styles had been comforting. "There are desks and boxes and filing cases of papers," Mother said. "We have made a little beginning, and by the time we have been through them all, perhaps we will know what really happened."

"Somebody must know," Dick said. "We just have to find that person."

It was not very late when they got home, and the three Miltons left behind were still up to wait for them. "You said we were not to do the dishes alone," Roddy said conscientiously, "and I have been thinking up a scheme. This kitchen and this sized family is just exactly right for it. Do you remember how we saw the production line in the Ford factory? Well, this is something like it. I was hoping that when I had sold enough minnows I could get us an electric dishwasher, but this will do until I think of something else."

Roddy's schemes were often very good, much better than the project for selling minnows. This was one of his best. He arranged the family in a row opposite the kitchen sink and its counters, and settled that one should stack, one should wash, one should rinse, one dry and put away. There was just the right amount of space and the right number of people. Even Bella, standing on a box, could dip the soapy plates into hot water; Mother or Dick, being the tallest, had to set the dishes on the shelves. The whole process went like clockwork from the very beginning. They had to change places now and again, for each one wanted to try what the other was doing. The dishes were clean and set in place in no time at all, and then everyone trooped up to bed.

Dick stood for a moment at his window, enjoying the view of the clustered lights of the village below, and the far twinkling ones of the farms spread out over the Champlain valley. Two of the windows looked out on far country, the third opened into the very branches of the great maple tree that stood by the house. So close it was that often, in the last few weeks, he had come in to find a gold or scarlet leaf laid carefully on his desk, as though put there by some friendly hand to show how beautiful was the world outside.

He was taking off his jacket, preparing for bed, when a sudden thought struck him. Hadn't he seen something that day, among the papers in the chest upstairs, which had something to do with what Mr. Styles had been saying? Certainly he could not go to sleep until he had looked. There was no electricity in the top story of the house, but there was a candle and a box of matches on the table at the foot of the attic stairs. He lighted it and went up quickly.

It was very dark and a little ghostly up there, but the air was fresh and dust-free after the vigorous cleaning the place had received earlier. The dim shapes of chests and trunks and boxes stood in orderly rows and he found his way quickly to the one into which he had been looking that morning when Martha Jenkins had been telling Anne about the patchwork quilt. He realized that he had been attending far more to the story than to the bundle of papers he had untied. He set the candle down carefully on a big box and began to look for a certain paper which had meant nothing to him when he had looked at it before, but might, after all, be something. He had just put his hand on it when he heard his mother coming up the stairs after him. "Dick," she asked, "what are you doing up here so late?"

He pulled out the paper and they read it together. "Copy of receipt given to Gerald Stewart for money put in my hands to invest. 15,000." The date was four years old. So the money concerned belonged to Jerry Stewart. Dick might have guessed it, he thought, but he was not sure.

"That's an opening," Mother said. "It gets us some-

where, but I have to say it doesn't get us very far."

"We can go on," Dick said. "Now we really know what to look for." He went to bed very happy and confident.

The weeks began to move quickly, and autumn was verging upon winter. There was a Saturday when Dick and Anne were in the attic again, she working on the quilt which, when finished after all the years, was to be her mother's Christmas present, he plodding through the bundles of papers but today finding nothing but ordinary bills. Letters were in other boxes; he had been through some of them and they absorbed him. The more he read the more he began to feel acquainted with his grandfather. "If only people thought about us the way they thought about him," Dick kept saying within himself. And was there any real reason why they shouldn't, why they would not think just the same of Mother — always friendly, always cheerful, working so hard, waiting without hard feeling for the people round about to begin to understand what the Milton family stood for? On this day he was to come to see that one person, at least, had learned to understand them.

They had seen nothing of Mrs. Jenkins who washed for Mrs. Towner next door, even though there had been one wash day of bad weather. This was another one, raw and cold and sleeting a little. Someone was coming up the stairs who certainly wasn't Mother; the door was pushed open and yes, there was Martha Jenkins once more with her heavy basket. Her round cheeks were apple red and her eyes snapped, but although Dick and Anne greeted her joyfully, for a few minutes she made little reply. She had got three wet sheets hung up before she said, "I expect you're surprised to see me here."

"We hoped you'd come back," Anne assured her, "But — how did it happen? Was Mrs. Towner away?"

"No, she was right there and having to listen to everything I had to say," Martha returned with energy. " 'I don't iron clothes that aren't dried right and proper,' I said to her. And she didn't answer so I just took up the basket and came. I said to her as I went out of the door, 'Why not let people do the right thing in their own way?' That's what I said. And I said, 'Anyone who spoke three words to Mrs. Milton and heard her answer would know that she would never stand for anything wrong. She's a real lady. And she's taught her children to do right, just the same way. And to be courteous to everyone, even strangers,' I said, 'even strangers who live next door and don't know a lady when they see one.' "

Martha Jenkins had evidently got so warm over her argument with Mrs. Towner that walking across the lawn in the cold sleet meant nothing to her. Anne helped her finish hanging the clothes and then took her over to show her how the quilt was getting on. "Now I never thought you could do it so nice," Martha exclaimed. "And you've got it not far from finished. When you've sewed the last patches together, my daughter and I will come and bring our big frame,

and quilt it with you." She told Anne what to buy
for lining and padding and then took her way downstairs with the empty basket. "I asked Mamie Towner
if she wanted to do her own washing," were her last
words, "and I think she's about decided by now."

Dick had fallen into the way of going up to the Usher
farm whenever he could find time, for he enjoyed Sam
Usher and liked to help him with the farm chores. He
was interested to see all that had to be done to get a
farm ready for the winter — cutting wood, banking
the north side of houses to keep the cold out, filling
the cellar with potatoes and cabbages buried in sand.
But he did not often go into the house. Mrs. Usher's
manner to him never changed, and he always felt
chilled and uncomfortable when he came near her. But
they were all very busy at home and he could not
manage to go as often as he would have liked.

One afternoon when Dick and Roddy had gone into
the Higgins hardware store to buy turpentine and
white lead, Mr. Higgins, the owner, for the first time
offered a remark beyond, "This is the best quality," or
"We have no other shade than this." He said, "It strikes
me you two boys are buying a lot of paint."

"A big house needs a lot of paint," Dick said. "The
whole inside needs doing over."

"And you're painting it yourselves?" Mr. Higgins
asked, evidently interested in spite of himself.

Dick nodded. "Mother and Roddy and me," he
answered. "The girls can help some; they wash off
the old paint before we go over it."

"It always was a sightly place," Mr. Higgins said. "I used to go there to deliver things, ever since I began in this store as errand boy. Your grandfather, Mr. Devons, didn't seem to notice much that it was getting shabby, but I used to wish I could see that nice woodwork all white again." Something seemed to have aroused Mr. Higgins' curiosity, for when the boys had collected their bucket of white lead and jugs of turpentine, he announced suddenly, "That's a lot of heavy stuff for two boys to carry. I'll take you over in the pick-up." He wrote on a slate at the door, "Back soon." took the heaviest jug and they bumped away.

He came into the wide hall and stood looking at it, fresh and clean with its new paint, and with the newly polished dark steps of the stairs coming down to it. "You've certainly done well," he exclaimed, almost in spite of himself. "We wouldn't any of us have ever thought that city people would work so hard over an old house in a village. There's Roger Devons' tall clock on the landing, just the way it used to be. I repaired the weights for him once." He gave Mother a glance of admiration, and hurried off, shoving the money into his pocket.

Once when Dick had gone to Mr. Styles' office with a message from his mother, Mr. Styles detained him for a minute before he left. "It's getting into December," he said, "and I think I should tell you that it is a custom hereabouts that, if someone comes to your door and asks to cut a Christmas tree on your land, you let them."

Dick had been having a hard and weary day, and for the first time he spoke bitterly. "Do you think that there is anyone here who would ever ask us?" he said.

Mr. Styles looked at him over his glasses. "They might," he returned. "They just might."

And Andrew Styles was right for, as they came into the week before Christmas, there was one afternoon a knock at the door and when Dick opened it, a little boy was there.

"I'm Bobby Higgins," he said with a cheery grin. "My grandfather, down at the hardware store, thought maybe you would let me get a Christmas tree up on your hill back of the house. I brought my hatchet to cut it." Evidently Bobby Higgins was not asking for a very big one, for his hatchet looked as though it was the one George Washington was said to have used on the cherry tree.

"We'll help you get it," Dick agreed heartily, and the whole Milton family turned out with sleds and hatchets and ropes to get him as fine a tree as the hill afforded. They cut him a lusty round one and helped him drag it home to his house, smelling cold and spicy and delicious as they carried it up the steps of the back porch to wait for the great day.

Their own tree took a great deal of choosing and arguing about, but at last it was cut, brought home and set up in the hall, a big and beautiful one, straight as an arrow, that reached the ceiling. Everyone was making things in corners and the air was thick

with mysteries. A whole clothes-basket full of presents
was gathering in the big closet under the stairs. Mother
had been very tactfully blind to the activities going
on in the attic, where her present from Anne was
being completed. It is remarkable how much a person
can keep from seeing if she really tries.

A good number of the presents that had been pre-
pared were for the Ushers, whose Christmas, they all
knew, would not be a very bountiful one. It was part
of the plan of their first Christmas celebration in
Jefferson that, on the afternoon of Christmas Eve,
they would go up the hill together, the little girls
and all, to take the Ushers their gifts and wish them a
Merry Christmas.

It was a gray afternoon, with some snow on the
ground, but not too cold, when they made ready to
set out. Everyone had something to finish or a last
package to wrap, so that they were later in starting
than they had intended. "We won't stay long," they
decided. The little girls wanted to tramp the whole
of the way on their snowshoes, but Mother said it
was too far.

"Perhaps we can't make it the whole way in the
station wagon, through this snow," she said. The rough
twisting road was never very easy going at best and,
after all, an old station wagon cannot do everything.
"So you can take your snowshoes," she directed. "You
may be able to use them for the last part of the way."

The faithful car groaned and creaked and climbed
but at last, rounding a steep turn, it began spinning

its wheels and digging into the snow rather than going forward. Mother backed and tried again, but in the end got one wheel halfway down into the ditch so that they must give it up. "Perhaps Sam and Mr. Usher will come down and help us get going on the way home," she said. "It isn't much farther is it? So the girls can use their snowshoes."

It had snowed often and easily in the last few weeks and it was hardly a surprise to them when snow began to come down once more. But today it was not quite like what they had got used to. The flakes were smaller and fell, straight down, with no wind, coming faster and faster and faster. It seemed, presently, as though they were in a white tent which traveled with them. All the children were delighted with it, making snowballs; the girls looking back to see their strange arrow-shaped tracks coming along behind them.

"How fast they get covered up," Anne said. They tucked the Usher packages under their coats and climbed steadily on.

But now the light was failing all around them, even though they were wrapped in the thick curtain of white. The whole air seemed to be moving down, down. Mother stumbled over a big stone and almost fell, Anne caught her snowshoe on a stump. "Dick," Mother said, "we're off the road."

It was quite true, but by a little moving back and forth they got on to it again. Yet the deep ruts that marked it were disappearing very fast. Bella stumbled now, then suddenly stood still and began to cry. "I'm

cold," she sobbed. "I don't want to go any farther."
Anne agreed with her and was near tears, too, as she
said, "Let's go home."

Mother looked at Dick and Roddy, their faces very
round and red and anxious as they looked up at her.
"We may have come too far for that," she said, with a
little catch in her voice. They all stood still, Anne with
her face hidden in her mother's skirt.

Mother's eyes met Dick's squarely. "You know this
road better than any of us," she said. "You are the only
one to tell whether we are near enough to the top to
go on, or ought we to turn back."

Dick felt a quiver inside of him, answering to the
catch in Mother's voice. How strange it was that on an
ordinary afternoon and on an ordinary errand, all of
a sudden there was something to be frightened about.
Mother's voice went on, it was steady now.

"Dick, you will have to decide."

CHAPTER FIVE

Roddy at the Auction

There was no way that Dick could have told his mother just how he knew exactly where they were on the steep, snowy road. Some shadow of a big rock looming through the thick flakes, some rougher track under foot must have told him without his being sure whence the knowledge came. But he answered his mother with confidence.

"We are pretty well up the hill and we have to go on. The girls — no, not even the rest of us — could make it, if we tried to go down."

He took off Bella's snowshoes, too small for anyone

else, and left them standing up in the snow at the
edge of the road. He lifted her to his shoulders
for it was plain that she could not walk any farther.
He stumbled a little before he got his balance and
then trudged on. Anne caught hold of her mother's
skirts and Roddy took her hand. With every minute
it seemed that the snow was falling thicker and thicker.

Nobody said a word as they tramped on, going
always slower and a little slower. At last Dick stood
still. "We're not far away now," he said. "Let's all of
us shout at the same time. One, two, three, HALLOO."
He would not have willingly told anyone, but he knew
that he could not carry his little sister any farther.

Their voices sounded lost in the thick-falling snow,
but nonetheless Dick thought that the Ushers heard.
"They must have heard," he told himself fiercely. He
could think of them, all inside the house, suddenly
listening for something, they could not know what.
Country people are quick at harkening to any new
sound. They know that every noise of any kind means
something. Sam would go to the door and open it to
hear better. "Now," Dick said. "Again, all of us.
HALLOO."

There was a breath of waiting and then an answer,
very small through the snow. "Halloo."

In what seemed the least possible time they caught
sight of a bobbing lantern and heard the swish of
skis. Nora and Sam Usher came suddenly through the
white curtain. Dick heard Mother's deep breath of
relief that was almost a sob. The two Ushers took off

their skis, which were not too good for going uphill, and set them up carefully beyond the edge of the road. Nora took Bella on her back and Sam, with the lantern swinging from his arm, picked up Anne. Mother took hold of Dick's belt and Roddy took hold of hers. They moved on, in single file, up and up, around a turn and up again and then were suddenly at the big doorstone and Mrs. Usher was opening the door. She seemed too much surprised to say a word, even of greeting. Mother untied the scarf from her hair and shook the snow out of it.

"We've come to wish you a Merry Christmas," she said.

Little Betsey Usher was jumping up and down in the excitement of having Anne and Bella Milton come to see her. The Christmas packages had not suffered much, having been well buttoned up under coats or inside pockets. Piled up on a table in the corner they made a fine showing of ribbon and holly and gay greeting cards. Mrs. Usher, even though she was more cheerful than they had even seen her before, said very little as she hurried about, mixing batter cakes, pouring out glasses of milk, and heating maple sirup. Boots and jackets were taken off to be dried, half-frozen fingers and feet were warmed by the stove, everyone except Mrs. Usher laughed and talked and made merry. But even she was smiling and asking people if they would have more batter cakes and were they warm yet.

At last, after they had talked and eaten and pushed

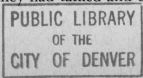

back their chairs, Dick went to the window to look at the weather. The snow was thinner now, though it was still falling, and the short afternoon twilight was almost at an end. Mr. Usher came over to look beside him.

"It don't look so bad as it did," he commented cheerily. "Sam will help me shovel the garage door free and I'll get out the car to take you down. It is the littlest and the oldest car in three townships, but it can carry you all just the same."

"But how could you ever get back up the hill?" Dick asked.

"Oh, the snow plough will be out presently," Sam's father said. "I can make it all right. But it makes me shiver to think that you, the little girls and all, walked up that hill in the face of the storm."

They were standing up to say good-bye, winding on their mufflers and pulling on their mittens. Mother went over to Mrs. Usher.

"I want to say something that I should have said long ago," she said. "It wasn't until Mr. Styles told me that I realized that I — that I am your landlord. I wanted to say that you are not to mind about the rent. Not until things go well with you again. And have a good Christmas."

Dick heard Mrs. Usher give a great quivering sigh, he certainly also saw tears standing in her eyes. Her face was working but she drew herself up. "We can't willingly take charity," she said.

"It isn't charity," Mother answered with authority.

"You are to be our guests, and my father's guests. He was such a friend to you that he would not have wanted it to be any other way."

Mrs. Usher's face changed queerly when Mother spoke of her father, Dick noticed. It was almost as though she looked frightened. She bowed her head to agree to Mother's offer, but she could not get out a word of thanks.

Meanwhile the little car had come chugging through the snow, its noisy engine and its lights working bravely. The Miltons climbed in; there was just exactly room for all of them. Dick was sure that Mother, in the back seat, shut her eyes at the beginning of the way down and did not open them again until they were on level ground and at the edge of the village. They passed the station wagon tilted forlornly in the deep rut and shapeless in its covering of snow. Dick touched his mother's arm as they got to the foot of the road, and said, "It's all right now." More than once the little car had slid like a toboggan, but it had never got out of Joe Usher's control. If it was the oldest car in three townships, Mother said later, he was the best driver in five states.

When they got fairly into the village street they saw a group of lights before them and a crowd of men, moving slowly along together. It was the snow plough advancing with its helpers, who shoveled the snow from the crossings where they were blocked by the high white ridges. Behind the plough the street was packed smooth and shiny, a winding white ribbon of snow where the big wheels had passed. Mr. Usher backed into their driveway to let them out.

"If you'll give me your car keys," he said, "one of the village men will get the station wagon out and bring it down to you. And I'll never forget your coming up the mountain to bring my children presents and to carry us that message about the farm. A good Christmas to you, though I know it is no easy one with your husband so far away. Good night."

The big house had never looked lovelier than it did at the moment when they came in. It was dressed in its Christmas greens, the tree tall and fragrant beside the stairs, a few red coals left in the burned out fire in the dining room. It was soon all noise and bustle and laughter, with much scampering backward and forward to get coats and mittens put away and to make supper ready.

They were in the midst of it when there was a thump on the door knocker and Roddy went to open it. Mr. Jones of the express office was there, his face very wet and shiny from the cold and the snow. "This box came in on the last train," he said. "It looks like it has traveled a long way so I brought it up as I was going home. No, there's no thanks due, its just in the line of business." He went off whistling into the dark.

They had quite finished supper and the little girls were so tired they were almost asleep at the table, when the knocker sounded again, and the door was opened, a little timidly, for their neighbor, Mrs.

Towner, to come in. She stood in the hallway, looking embarrassed and doubtful and then explained all in a rush. "Joe Usher stopped at my house to wish me Merry Christmas before he went back up the mountain. He told me what all of you did, coming up in the snow to bring presents to his children." Her face still looked severe, almost as though she did not approve, but Dick realized suddenly that it was because she had that kind of a face. "I thought — I got thinking about how you go to church so regularly Sundays and that most likely you would be wanting to go tonight, to the midnight service, since you attend the Episcopal church, isn't that right? And I thought maybe you'd like me to come over and stay with the little girls while you and the boys go. Would you?" She had said it all in one breath, as though if she paused she could not go on again.

Mother stood too astonished to speak for an instant, then went across and threw her arms about Mrs. Towner's neck and kissed her. "Bless you," she said. The lady looked very much surprised; it was certainly a long time since she had been kissed. For a minute her face did not change, then it creased into a truly warm smile.

"Martha Jenkins was certainly right about you, but I didn't believe her. Now that I know what you are really like, there isn't anything I wouldn't do for good neighbors. It isn't any favor. I can go to my own church in the morning. Let's get these sleepy little girls to bed."

In the end Roddy was so tired that he also had to be tucked into bed and it was only Mother and Dick who left Mrs. Towner in the big rocking chair by the fire and went off through the white streets. There were candles in the windows everywhere, so that the whole town was full of the gentle yellow glow of Christmas light, and the tall, colored windows of the little Episcopal church made bright pictures against the dark. Inside it was spicy with the smell of pine and juniper, and crowded. The deep organ was just beginning "O little town of Bethlehem," as they came in.

As he sat very still, but very wide awake, Dick looked at his mother and thought how pretty she was in her brown fur hat and fur-collared coat, yet how tired her face was. She looked sad, too; something one ought not to be at Christmas. He knew, as he had not stopped to realize before, how hard it was for her with Daddy so far away and for such a long time. They missed him, too, all of his children, but they had been too busy to feel sad. Dick moved over a little closer to his mother, and she smiled down at him and did not look sad any more. He saw Mr. Styles' smooth silver head a few pews in front of them and he even thought that, away down in front, he caught a glimpse of Jerry Stewart, but he was not sure. On the steep block above them the Congregational church struck twelve. Christmas was coming in.

The next day, of course, was all confusion and shouting of Merry Christmas, of emptying stockings and opening presents and calling out, "Oh, look, look at this," while everyone dutifully tried to look at everything at once and did not succeed. The big box which had arrived last night was, naturally, from Daddy and out of it came wonders—queer Indian dolls for the girls, two beautiful braided belts for the boys, a smooth silver bowl for Mother, and scarves and embroideries for everyone. Dinner was enormous and jolly and noisy. Dick looked up and down the table. It was the first Christmas that he could ever remember when they had not had guests. "Well," he thought sturdily. "Five is a good many. It ought to be enough."

But they were to have guests, just the same. After dinner was over, the house had grown rather too hot and Roddy had set the front door open a little. Presently there came in, first, a beautiful yellow collie dog, waving a feathery tail and with snow flakes sprinkled along his back. On the threshold stood a tall man, knocking snow off his blue woolen cap and already feeling in the pockets of his leather coat. There was a real Christmas smile on his thin face. "Jerry," cried out Dick, forgetting that this was really Mr. Stewart whom he had only seen once before.

Jerry Stewart and Chris seemed very glad to be made so welcome; they were introduced to Mother and the others. Jerry began at once to bring presents out of all his pockets. Bella got a carved, fluttering bird that you blew into for a whistle, Anne a little music box, Roddy a pocket knife whose blades came out when you pressed a button, Dick a book. The square package for Mother looked very mysterious. On being unwrapped it turned out to be a round cake-stand, which revolved and played a tune, "Happy Birthday to you." Around the edges a set of names were carved, Dick, Roddy, Anne and Bella. "I thought a family with so many birthdays ought to have something permanent like this," Jerry explained.

He looked about at the spotless room, the bright curtains, the soft rugs and the shining floors and said, "How did you ever do it amongst you?" He turned to ask Dick, "Which room is yours? The one that looks out into the maple tree?"

"I am going to get you a cup of coffee," Mother said and vanished into the kitchen. Dick followed her a moment later to carry in the tray. She had set the kettle on to boil, but she was not doing anything else, only standing at the kitchen window, with her fingers on the sill, looking out at the snowy garden. He expected her to say something about their guest and she did.

"He knows every inch of the house, doesn't he?" she said. "Even if we had not learned it from the paper that you found, we would know that he was your grandfather's close friend, that it was his money my father undertook to care for." Dick nodded without surprise.

"I had been thinking that, too, from the time he came in."

"And if it is rightly his house," Mother went back to the thought which had evidently been going over and over in her mind ever since that night they first talked to Mr. Styles, "if it really ought to be his, we must give it to him."

"He would never take it," Dick protested.

"I would never keep it," Mother answered, her voice sounding, as it so seldom did, really stern.

The boy looked out of the window, at the snow in the little front garden, at the small dark cedar trees, the bare rosebushes, the gate with its posts topped with round caps of white. It seemed to him that he had never loved the place so much before as at that minute. "Surely," he begged, "there must be some answer; Mr. Styles said there was bound to be an answer. Somebody, somewhere, must know what became of Jerry's money."

"We can go on looking," his mother said. "We haven't been through all the boxes and drawers of papers yet. Everything we find and read seems to say the same thing—that your grandfather was the truest and most honest man that ever lived. But that is not enough; we knew that anyway." She drew a long breath. "We'll give ourselves a little more time. If we cannot find out what the truth is by the first of June, then we will give the house up and no power on earth can make me take it back again. But we will take that much time to make sure. And we will go on looking and working just as we wrote to Daddy that we were going to do."

She turned about from the window to make the coffee and set the pot on the tray. Dick picked it up and carried it in to Jerry by the fire, while his mother followed with the cakes.

Christmas went by and at New Year's came the wonderful surprise. There was a telegram from Daddy, saying that he was ordered back to Washington for a week to report on his work and that he could have three days to come up to visit them. They met him at the airport thirty miles away, and could hardly believe that he was really coming until he got out of the plane, tall, good looking and as excited as they were over the visit. They whirled him home, they took him all over the house, they showed him so many things and told him so many others between Friday and Monday that it was a wonder that he did not stop his ears.

It was not until the last evening that they really explained what was troubling them so much. "The people in Jefferson think that the house oughtn't to be ours," Dick said, but in his heart, as he said the very words he was more sure than ever that it was rightfully their own. But Mother only said again,

"We are giving ourselves six months to find out. We are not going to stop looking and watching for a minute in all that time. And we are going to go on working on the house, because any family, even if they are going away in the end, should leave a house better than they found it. And no matter what people may be thinking, we are going to be part of the town, and work and act as though we really belong here. Because we do."

The visit was over so quickly that it was hard to believe, when Daddy was gone, that he had really been there. School began again and time was slipping by quickly as it always does with busy people. The children had an Aunt Mary Milton who lived in Maine and who, every year, sent each of them, Mother included, a Christmas present of a new, rustling five dollar bill. "You children grow bigger so fast," her letters said, "that there is no way for an old woman like me to know what you might want. So go out and buy yourself, each one of you, something that you couldn't have had otherwise." It was also a habit that they waited quite a number of weeks to spend the money, having the fun of planning, deciding, changing their minds and deciding again, until the whole sum was spent.

There was more snow and then the finest of skating on the river. It got to be March and things began to thaw a little. Then Mother had an idea. "Mr. Hobbs is going to have an auction," she said. "Suppose we wait until then and buy our Aunt Mary Christmas presents there." They all agreed.

An auction in the very early spring is not so crowded as one in summer when tourists and visitors come to it, but Mr. Hobbs, who was going to live with his daughter in Canada and must empty his house, did not want to wait. "Everything has to go," he kept saying in his high, old voice. "They have served me, it will give me pleasure to have them begin to serve others." The whole family of Miltons made one trip to the house to look over everything that was to be sold, and to decide what they wanted. Roddy went several times; it was hard for him to make up his mind and he wanted to be sure that he had seen everything.

It was a pleasant day, with patches of snow still lying on Mr. Hobbs' grass, and buds showing on his big elm trees, where someone, so he said, had seen a robin. It was warm enough to stand outside and everyone crowded close as the auctioneer began calling out the different things for sale. "What do you bid, ladies and gentlemen, what do I hear bid? One dollar? Make it two. Two dollars? Make it four."

Mother got a pile of thin white plates with blue flowers. The top two were chipped so no one seemed to know that the rest were whole and something quite rare and beautiful. The little girls bought things, too, though Mother and Dick had to bid for them; Anne had a doll's bedstead, and Bella a doll's cradle, painted dark red with round wooden rockers. There was a little patchwork quilt still in it, just the right size. Dick got a box of books "That might have just almost anything in it," and did have a whole set of little red volumes called *The Franconia Stories,* written a hundred years ago, which later the whole family read and learned to love.

But Roddy was very hard to satisfy. He offered a bid once on a carpenter's bench, but it went up to fifteen dollars and so got out of his reach. Another time he was going to offer a dollar on a saw, but the man next to him warned, "That one isn't any good, sonny. It's rusted through and besides it's too big for you. Don't waste even a quarter on it." It finally was sold for fifteen cents and Roddy, looking at it later, was glad he had been saved from making such a mistake.

Time was going by, Mother was getting tired and the little girls were restless. Even Dick wanted to go home. But Roddy was not content to leave. "I've seen a few other things I want to bid on," he insisted.

"Let him stay here by me," said the man who had advised him about the saw. "I'll see he gets safe out of the crowd and home. The auction can't last more than another hour." So, since all of them were worn out because auctions can be very tiring, the four Miltons went home and left Roddy, still standing and watching for what would come next.

Mother went into the kitchen to get lunch; the girls were washing off their doll's furniture and trying their dolls in it. Dick had gone upstairs to wipe off the little red books and set them on his shelf, next to the King Arthur that Jerry Stewart had brought him. He heard cars going past and knew that the auction was over and people were starting home. Suddenly he heard a great rattling and snorting — the noise of a big truck turning and backing into their driveway.

"All the way up to the outside cellar steps," he heard Roddy directing a driver. "You will have to drive all the way in."

"We sure do," a man's voice answered. "This here

little purchase of yours weighs the best part of five hundred pounds."

Mother had opened the kitchen door and Dick heard her shocked voice, "Roddy, what in the world is this? What have you bought?" Roddy called up joyfully to his brother, "Dick — Dick, come down and look at what I've got."

CHAPTER SIX

The Cold Hills

The men on the truck got down and opened the wide wooden doors that covered the steps down to the cellar. The mass of dark metal braced in the body of the truck looked almost too heavy for any force of men, even these husky ones, to be able to move.

"It's a printing press," Roddy announced proudly. "It was in old Mr. Hobbs's cellar and he seemed awfully glad to get rid of it. Only the junk man bid against me, and he didn't go above three dollars and a half. I got it for four, and I wouldn't have bought it only these men said they would deliver it for a dollar."

A very large dollar's worth of effort it was that

finally managed to back the truck up to the cellar door and roll out the great heavy press.

"Are you sure," one of the men said to Mother who had come out to stand on the kitchen step, "are you sure you're willing to have it go down into your basement? Like as not it will never come out again."

"Yes, I'm quite willing," she assured him, and Roddy beamed at being so thoroughly understood.

"I always wanted a printing press," he said. "I didn't know they were so easy to get. And I'm going to start a paper and call it the *Jefferson Journal*. I thought it all up when the bidding began."

The little girls had come running out; Mrs. Towner, passing the gate, had been unable to resist coming in. The men were very skillful as they eased their enormous burden down the steps, asked Roddy respectfully where he would like it set, received their dollar and got into the truck laughing. "We thought if the little fellow had spunk enough to buy it, we could at least manage to deliver it for him," they said, and departed.

"Roddy, do you know how to print?" Mrs. Towner asked.

"No," he returned, untroubled. "I'm going to set out tomorrow and find somebody who can teach me."

As it proved, Roddy did not even have to look for a person to show him how to run the printing press, the teacher of printing came to look for him. The very next morning a young man drove up to the door, a very young man with dark-rimmed glasses and a portfolio of papers under his arm.

"I'm Professor Beckett from over at Highland College," he said. "At least I'm Tom Beckett and I'm interested in printing. I kept hearing about a very old press, almost the oldest in the state, and I'd been looking for it for years, and at last I heard Mr. Hobbs had it, had taken it for a debt forty years ago. By the time I got wind of the auction and got over here to Jefferson it was sold." He grinned. "Everyone in town was ready to tell me who bought it."

He was a nice boy; he did not seem like much more than a boy, and he spoke of knowing Jerry Stewart and his having said it would be all right to go up to see the press. He explained that Highland College was getting ready for its hundred and fiftieth anniversary celebration and he had been experimenting with printing a program which would look like the first one, got out in 1805. Would Roddy mind if he had a try at setting up something on the press here, even though it did not date back quite so far as that.

"There's a lot to do to it," he said happily. "It hasn't been cleaned or oiled, I should say, for well over forty years. Look, here's some of the old type came with it, even some long s's that look like f's. Do you mind if we begin now?"

Roddy's eyes were shining. No one could begin on his printing press too soon. "It's a monster, for such an old one," said Tom Beckett, taking off his coat.

He stayed all day, he stayed to dinner that night, he stayed all night finally and for the whole week end. He taught Roddy and Dick a great deal and he brought an unexpected addition to their printer's company. Something was wrong, on the second day, with the moving of some of the press's parts and Tom Beckett said, "I know the very fellow to set it right. He came over to Highland once with your high school science teacher to help us with some apparatus in the laboratory. He doesn't know too much about science yet, and perhaps nothing at all about printing, but he's the best mechanic I have ever seen." He hastened out to his car, was gone half an hour and came back with Rob Dale.

Not even Rob had known, apparently, where Tom Beckett was bringing him, and he stood hesitating on the threshold of the basement door when Tom sought to hurry him in. Roddy spoke up to give him warm welcome. The boy knew something of his brother's bad moment with young Dale, but to Roddy nothing was important where his printing press was concerned. Dick came forward a moment later. "We'll be glad of your help," he said and Rob went to work.

Tom Beckett had to get up before sunrise to drive back to Highland and his classes on Monday morning, but he carried the proof of a very respectable announcement for the college's coming celebration. He came back the next week and the next; Jerry Stewart came, in the end, to help, and the whole Milton family lent a hand when the double page program of the Highland ceremonies was finally run off. Rob Dale was called in more than once, when old and corroded parts stuck obstinately; he could always tinker at

them with success. And, a little later, after Roddy and Dick had carried out two weeks of hard, excited and inky work, there appeared the *Jefferson Journal*, "Number 1. Founded April 14th, 1955, by R. Milton. First number, April 14th, 1955, Editor R. Milton. Price free." It was but a single sheet, yet it had real news, a barn had burned down beyond the edge of the village: "At four o'clock it seemed to be doomed — but it wasn't, it was saved." A Persian kitten had been found and was being held (in the Milton basement, meowing loudly for its home) until it should be claimed by its owner. The bulldozers had begun digging for the new postoffice.

Every person in Roddy's part of the school got one and every week there were rising numbers of requests for more. A great many people laughed about the *J.J.* as it came to be called, but every child in school took his copy home where it was read by the grownups. Being printed on the spot it was a good rival to the ordinary village paper, the *News,* which always had to be sent to be printed in Champlain City before it could come out, and so was usually one step behind the news which everyone was telling everyone else in the post office, while the mail was being sorted.

Getting out the paper was hard work and took all of Roddy's time outside of school and his homework, and took also a good deal of Dick's, for the older boy was always ready to help the younger one in carrying out his cherished projects. Roddy had another volunteer assistant in Rob Dale, who had fallen into the

habit of drifting in once at least during every final ses-
sion with the weekly paper, to make sure that no me-
chanical breakdown was going to hold up the *J.J.* He
said very little, he never seemed to expect or want any
thanks, yet he made himself, somehow, a part of the
Jefferson Journal's staff.

Dick's own task was a much more difficult one, that
of solving the problem of what had become of Jerry
Stewart's money. He and his mother had gone through
stacks of papers of every sort, for the house held
hundreds of them. Each time that they were ready
to admit that there was no use in looking further,
some small bit of evidence would appear and spur
them to further toil. Dick had found the first one,
the copy of the receipt Roger Devons had given for
the money. Jerry Stewart, on seeing it, had recollected
that Mr. Devons had, indeed, given him such a paper,
but in all his comings and goings in the far Pacific,
with many changes of ships and quarters, it was not
so surprising that he had mislaid it. It was Mother
who came across the next one, a scrawl in her father's
very casual diary which said, "Going to New York
about J.S.'s investment. Amount now $17000." There
might be some doubt as to whether the initials really
were J.S. but Mr. Andrew Styles said that he felt
sure that they were. The money would probably be
increased in Roger Devons' very able hands, he explained.

On another day, when Dick and his mother had met
Mr. Styles at the bank for the purpose of going through

Roger Devons' strong box, it was Dick whose sharp
eyes caught sight of the scrap of paper caught between
two large legal envelopes. It said only, in hasty writing:
"J.S. Bonds, 18,560." It was evidently a label, but
what sort of a bundle it had fallen from there was no
way of guessing now. They came to the end of their
search and found nothing more.

"It's so easy for papers to go astray and disappear,"
Andrew Styles said with a sigh. "Half a dozen lines
would be enough for us, but the page they are written
on can so easily be lost for good."

"But it's not just set down on paper," Dick insisted.
He had given so much thought to the whole question
that there were certain matters of which he was
strangely sure. "It doesn't all depend on something
written. There is surely somebody who knows, besides
Grandfather — who saw the bonds, or heard him say
what he had done with them. And a person doesn't
disappear, like a page of paper. But we do need to
know who the person is," he admitted at the end.

No matter how difficult the task seemed to be, no
matter how plainly he saw that Mother was growing
discouraged, the more determined he became that
the solution must be found. "There is always an
answer, somewhere," Andrew Styles had said more than
once and to that Dick added, "There is always somebody, somewhere, who knows that answer." It was on
the afternoon after they had been to the bank that
Dick came down into the basement at home, where
Roddy was working at the press in the failing light.

"Do you know what I would like to do?" Dick said to his brother. "I would like to make one whole number of the paper just a single advertisement. 'Wanted, the person who knows where Jerry's money went,' printed in the biggest type you have."

"We couldn't do that," Roddy answered seriously. Dick knew well that they could not, that people did not advertise about family problems and that Mother would be horrified at the very thought. It was only at that moment that he saw that Rob Dale was there, standing by the door putting on his coat. He did not seem to have heard, however, for he said nothing except good night and went out. Roddy was too much interested in his paper to think more of what Dick had said. "I've got too much news," he complained. "I don't know how to get it all in."

There is a certain part of the early spring that people in New England call mud time, and have good reason for doing so. It rains and freezes a little, thaws, and rains again. The gravel roads are passable enough, but the fields and orchards are too soft and wet for any work to be done in them. This spring it had rained more than anyone could reasonably expect, it began to be time to plough and sow and nothing could be done. "A little more time given us before hard work starts," some people tried to say cheerfully, although many were beginning to look anxious.

It was perhaps because they had got tired of seeing their parents worrying and waiting that the 4-H Club boys and girls had got up a show of their calves over near Highland, and everybody who had a car or a friend who had an extra seat in one, decided to go. The bad weather moderated a little so that early in the afternoon everyone got off in high spirits. School closed at noon that day and car after car, crowded to the roof, went rolling down the road. No one had said anything to the Miltons about coming. It was just that no one seemed to have thought of it. They could have gone anyway, of course, but there seemed no great temptation to do so. The town certainly seemed very quiet as the four of them came home from school and went in soberly to get their lunch.

It was late in the afternoon when the rain came on again, torrents of it, sheets of it, thundering on the roof and pouring off the eaves in rivers. "The calf show will be under cover in the 4-H Club building," Mother said. "The Governor is coming to give out the prizes; that will be in the evening. There were to be shows and entertainments later, and by that time we'll hope that the rain will have stopped."

It was very surprising that they should have a visitor, but it was just after dark that there was a knocking at the front door. It was Mr. Higgins who came in, the man who owned the hardware store and also was one of the village managers — a selectman he was called. There was a friend with him, a selectman too, so it turned out. Both stood dripping with water in the middle of the hall.

"There hasn't been anything like this rain in ten years," Mr. Higgins said, taking his hat to the door to spill the water out of its up-curved brim. It's melting the last snow on the higher mountains and bringing water in floods down all the streams. The creeks are getting up nearly to the floors of the bridges already. There's not more than half of them high enough to be really safe. We need to go out and set up warning signs to keep people off the bridges and mark roads as closed, but the bother of it is there's not enough signs."

"Yes?" Mother said. They were all waiting to know why these men had come to them.

"Not enough signs," Mr. Harris repeated. "And every man Jack away at Highland each with a car full of women and children coming home in the dark, near midnight. And me out of black paint down at the store for lettering signs and not too much of white, either, for painting new ones. John West and I came up to see if you had any paint to spare, I know you've been buying it pretty steady all winter. That last lot you couldn't have used up yet. I thought you'd bought more black than you were ever going to need, but I didn't say so."

"You can come down into the basement and look," Mrs. Milton said. "All the extra supply we have is there and you are welcome to every bit of it. And if there's painting to do, why my boys and I are pretty good with brushes."

The two men, their boots still squelching with water, went down the steep stairs with them to the workshop in the basement. How lucky it was that

Mother had always made the boys keep it tidy. The visitors looked with respect at the printing press that took up the whole of one wall, but their eyes went at once to the row of paint cans in the corner. "Now Higgins, look at that," John West said in relief.

Dick had been planning to make a new bookcase for his room and he had set up a row of beautifully white-painted shelves against the wall to dry.

"Say," said Mr. Higgins, "if I would block out the lettering do you think you could fill it in with black, and get the signs ready while we go out to set them up? There's just not a minute to lose; some of the places where we need them worst are ten or fifteen miles away."

There was no need even to answer. The boys were plunging into their overalls, Mr. Higgins was down on his knees with a stubby black pencil in his hand, Mother was mixing up paint and setting out brushes. Dick had the first two done while Mr. Higgins was marking out the others. The men brought in stakes for them, out of the pick-up truck in which they had come, and the two nailed and hammered while the Miltons painted. Mr. Higgins, although he had run short of black paint, had fortunately a store of the shiny-headed nails that can be put on signs to make them glimmer in the dark when car lights fall upon them. In less than an hour six signs were ready. Soaked as the two selectmen were, and without a word except to thank Mrs. Milton for a cup of coffee each, they went hurrying out into the pouring rain and the dark.

It was very still in the workshop now. Mother had got the girls to bed; she had put on her slacks and was painting too, they were all working for dear life. Suddenly there was a step on the cellar steps and Jerry Stewart came down. He had heard from the selectmen of what was going on and had come to help. He took three of the signs, finished now and saying, "Road Closed," or, "Bridge Unsafe," and went out to set them where he had been told that they were needed. A few of the higher bridges were quite safe, but the smaller ones on the side roads had wild water running close to the floor boards and no one should risk going over them. When he came back the selectmen were with him. They took the remaining signs with them and the beautiful bookcase shelves were gone to the last one.

Dick was counting up the places which they had managed to mark. "There's still the little bridge on the road that goes up to Mrs. Malvern's house," he told Jerry, and Jerry said to the selectmen:

"Dick is right, there is one more. And I heard that Mrs. Malvern was due to come up this week end, and she's not one to stop for a storm. And with that heavy car her chauffeur drives . . ."

"Well," answered Mr. Higgins doubtfully, "you'll have to make another sign and put it up. We must get out with these for the main road."

"The boys and I will put it up," Jerry assured them. "But we're going to have to be quick."

After the two men were gone Dick searched and

found a last board, painted white some time ago. Jerry set up the letters, "Bridge Unsafe," and Dick splashed on the paint while Jerry cut the stake to fasten the sign. "It wouldn't do to nail it to her post, they maybe wouldn't see it at the side of the road," he observed, grinning, and thinking of the day of the "Minnows for Sale."

Mother was willing that they should set it up and they put on boots and raincoats to go with Jerry in his car. The rain was not falling quite so heavily now, but even as they came out of the house they could hear the roar of all the little streams, that ran full and foaming, past Jefferson Village down to Lake Champlain. They went slowly and carefully down their own road, through the edge of the village, along the branch way that led to the bridge. Jerry had brought a hatchet; they cut a slot in the flooring and drove the signpost into it, to stand straight up in the middle of the way. In the dark, Dick peering down, thought he had never seen anything look more cruel and angry than the black water sweeping by just below the floor of the bridge. He could have put down his hand and touched it.

"We're not more than just in time," Jerry said. The lights of a big car had turned off the main road and were moving toward them. Jerry waved his flashlight, then shone it on the sign, and the car, which had been coming quickly, slowed down to a stop. Phillips, the chauffeur, got out and almost immediately a window was rolled down and Mrs. Malvern's voice came out of the darkness.

"What is this? What is the meaning of this? Phillips, why don't you go on?"

Phillips wanted to examine the bridge himself, so Jerry with the two boys walked back to explain to Mrs. Malvern. She had turned on the light inside the car and sat there in a fur jacket and glittery small hat, looking puzzled and angry. She seemed to take it as being somehow Jerry's fault, when he explained what had happened. "What do we pay taxes for if they can't keep their bridges up better than this?" she exclaimed angrily. The two boys came nearer, into the circle of light and she suddenly recognized them.

"You here still?" she cried out. "I thought you would have been gone by now."

Dick and Roddy slid back into the darkness. Phillips was coming to tell her that it would be impossible to take the heavy car over the bridge. Jerry was explaining, as patiently as he could, and when he could be heard through her indignation, that by going around twenty miles they could cross on a high bridge and so get home in due time.

"Then get in and start off at once," she snapped to Phillips, when even she saw that there was no good in arguing.

Phillips got in and began backing the car, for there was no room to turn round. The lights drew away from them, then stopped. Phillips got out and came back. "I — I'd like to shake your hand, sir," he said to Jerry, "for what you've done this night — for *her*." He jerked his head backward toward where Mrs. Malvern was waiting and fuming in the car.

"Shake hands with the boys instead," Jerry answered, pushing the two forward. "And ask them if they can excuse your mistress for her miserable temper."

"She's had things her own way always. It isn't good for people," Phillips returned, as he shook Dick's hand and then Roddy's. "But I know what you've done for her." He grinned. "She'll know it too tomorrow when she sees the bridge gone."

It was ten o'clock when they all got home again, tired, wet and splattered with mud. The girls, wide awake now, had crept downstairs to find out what was happening. Jerry came in only for a cup of coffee and a sandwich and then hurried away to help the selectmen finish their night's work.

The boys were having sandwiches, too, and a mug of cocoa each, and Dick was saying wearily, "I think we might just call it a day — " when there was again a sudden knocking at the door. It opened before anyone could go to it, and Mrs. Markley, Nadine's Aunt Cora, came in.

"Nadine is here, isn't she?" were her first words. Her voice sounded desperate. She tried to make her face stiff and formal, but it was working and the tears were running down. "I've looked for her at all my friends' houses, everywhere possible in the village, but I can't find her. If she isn't here — she's lost."

Even as she spoke a great gust of rain came battering against the windows and blowing in at the open door. All the Miltons were in the hall now, staring anxiously at their visitor.

"She didn't go to Highland with you?" Mrs. Milton asked.

"No, the Thompsons had room for only one extra in their car and Nadine said she didn't much want to go. She wanted to go home, there was a birthday or something up at their house, but I told her she couldn't hope to find anyone to take her when everybody was going over to the 4-H show at Highland. I had to get ready in a hurry and I couldn't attend much to what she was saying. I told her to go over to Jenny Morton's house and wait until I got back. I only got here half an hour ago and Jenny Morton says she was out at her mother's all afternoon and her house was empty. I guess about every house in the town was empty too. I hoped, maybe — even though I said different — that she might have come here."

"She hasn't been here," Mother said gently. There was no use in asking this proud and stubborn woman if she had not forbidden the little girl to come to her real friends, lest she be "taking favors from strangers." Bella and Anne had whispered together and Anne came forward now and touched her mother's arm. "I think," she said clearly, "that Nadine went home."

"Walking, and in all this rain? Oh surely that's not possible," her aunt cried out. But Anne stuck to her idea, and Bella upheld her. "Once she told me," Anne insisted, "that if she had to she could get home herself; she could walk up the hill path — it's shorter than the road — to Rob Dale's house and that probably he could get out his uncle's car and take her the rest of the way. She seemed to be very sure that he would."

"But maybe Rob and his uncle went to Highland. Everyone went to Highland." Cora Markley's voice was a cry of terror.

"Everyone but Nadine," Mrs. Milton reminded her. Her voice was still kind though it might have been very severe. "I believe Anne is right," she went on. "Nadine knew you did not want her to come here and ask us to take her home, and she must have felt that she was being left alone by everybody. She may have gone to a dozen doors and not found anyone. It couldn't have been raining so very much when she started out."

She picked up her leather jacket from where she had put it down when she last came in. "Dick," she said as though no one, now, had the right to be making plans but herself, "go over to Mrs. Towner's and tell her what has happened. I saw a light in her window and she must have got home. Ask her to come and stay with the girls while we go to look for Nadine. Tell her we might even have to be gone all night. And Mrs. Markley, you had better go back to your house; the child might have turned back and we don't want her to find any more doors closed when she knocks. The boys will go with me. I'm not very good at remembering roads, but they will know the way."

Mrs. Towner came at once. "I'll get the girls to bed again, and not let them worry," she promised.

Anne had followed her mother like a shadow. "Don't you think that maybe you need me to help look for Nadine," she begged. Mother bent to kiss her.

"We do need you, just as we needed you to guess where Nadine had gone," she assured her daughter. "But there mustn't be any more little girls out in the wind and rain tonight." She backed the car down the drive and they were away down the street.

Mother, as she had often said, "was very good at taking wrong turnings." But both the boys had excellent memories and a good sense of direction, so that they got out of the town and on the right road up the mountain without any delay. Dick thought he ought to walk up by the hill path, but Mother insisted that it would be quicker to drive up and ask at the Dale house if Nadine had been there. They could search the path later if need be.

Seen in the bright beam of the car headlights, the road seemed rougher than ever before, and, flowing with water as it was, there were times when Mother could hardly hold the car in the middle of the road. The rain slashed against the windshield and presently one of the wipers gave out with a squeak and wiped no more. Fortunately it was the one in front of Dick, so that his mother could still see. They met and passed one car only on the long climb upward, this, going in the opposite direction, was hurrying so fast that there was no chance to hail the driver and ask if he had seen

Nadine. It was not quite eleven o'clock when they pulled up at the door of the forlorn little house where Rob Dale lived.

Rob himself came to the door almost before they had stopped, and behind him they could see the untidy room and his mother looking in from the kitchen, a feeble oil lamp barely lighting the dreary place. They explained to Rob what had happened and he came out into the rain to hear more. His face, seen clearly now in the lights of the car, was deeply troubled. "You think Nadine came up here to look for me?" he said. "We've only been back here since ten minutes ago, my uncle who lives down the road a piece, came and took my mother and my sister and me to Highland for the afternoon. If Nadine came, she did not find anyone."

"Poor little mite," Mother said. "Do you think she could still be on the path coming up from the village?"

"There's been plenty of time for her to get here, and go on further up," Rob said. "Unless something has happened — ." He stopped to listen as though he had heard some new sound above the storm. "Let's get on as far as the bridge," he suggested. Not for a minute had he seemed to think anything except that finding Nadine was as much his affair as theirs.

Roddy, in the back seat, opened the door and Rob got in. Mother started slowly up the mounting road; it was steep here and made a turn. As they rounded the curve they could hear the little stream, swollen now to a torrent, shouting one minute then dropping its voice the next to seem to talk to itself. The lights came round and fell full upon the flooring of the bridge. In spite of herself Mother stopped.

The water was high but not yet nearly level with the bridge floor. Yet every few minutes a wave would come rolling down the stream and flow in a thin sheet over the middle of the bridge, then subside again. The rails on both sides stood firm. As they stopped and Mrs. Milton shut off the engine, there came a second of quiet when the sound of the wind dropped too and the noise of the water was not so loud.

"Did you hear it?" Dick said suddenly. "I am sure I heard something — somebody crying."

"I heard it too, even when we were down at the house," Rob said and jumped out as he spoke. He went forward, stepped on the planks of the bridge, stamped on them and found them steadier than he had thought and walked as far as the middle. "It's the stoutest of all the bridges around here," he said, "and it seems to be holding all right. The water isn't nearly up to the floor, its only a flood wave now and then that goes over. And I've driven my uncle's car across many's the time, with water running over like this. And we'll get up the hill quicker if we go in the car. Mrs. Milton, won't you all get out and let me take the car over?"

Mother smiled down into his earnest face and shook her head. "If the car goes on, I'm the one to drive it. And I think it should go on. Dick and Roddy must get out and one of you must stand over there on the other side to signal if I am going right."

It was Dick who went across, with the others ordered to wait until the car was over. Mother went slowly and carefully, a yard, another yard, she had passed the middle, she was coming into the road on the other side.

"It's all right," Dick called back to the other two. They started across; Mother opened the door and leaned out to watch them.

It may have been that the weight of the car was too much for the bridge, and had broken some beam or support below. Or it may have been that there was another and greater wave of flooding water coming down at that moment. There was a second when it seemed that the two were almost across in safety, then there came a sudden tearing and ripping of breaking boards and the whole floor of the bridge stood up on end, lurched to one side and went over into the black water. They could see Roddy, holding to the rail and then flung out clear of the mass of planks and beams. What had happened to Rob Dale they could not even see.

CHAPTER SEVEN

The Blue Heron

Dick was down at the edge of the stream, almost waist deep in water, holding to a tree to keep from being swept away and trying desperately to see what might be going on in that boiling blackness. All that he could catch sight of was dark circling shapes that might be anything, and white riffles of foaming water. Suddenly a light fell on the whole scene. Mother had managed, somehow, to back the car around so that the long beams of the headlights reached down to the water. He could see Roddy now, his head coming up among the floating planks, and he could also see Rob

Dale, emerging beside Roddy and flinging a strong arm around the smaller boy.

"I've got him," Rob shouted, and began to swim manfully toward shore.

"Here, here," shouted Dick at the top of his lungs, for the water was roaring again, "here's a flat place on the bank where you can get to land."

He waded out to meet them, feeling the stony bottom with his feet for one firm step after another. He got Roddy on the other side and together the two boys brought him to the bank.

"I'm — I'm all right," Roddy mumbled, "only pretty full of water." He sputtered out a good deal of it and shook the wet hair out of his eyes. They stood together and watched the remains of the bridge go heaving and tumbling downstream. The whole mishap had taken only a few seconds.

Mother was running down the bank to them; she gave a cry of relief when she saw the three of them standing there together. There was little said as they went up the slope to the car. "Rob will have to turn it around for me," Mother said. "I have no idea how I got it turned the first time. And how is Rob going to get back across the brook?"

"I'm going on up with you," Rob said briefly. "We've got to find Nadine."

He turned the car neatly and, at a sign from Mrs. Milton, stayed at the wheel as they went up the next rise in the road, peering into the darkness on each side. They had been right; it was true that they had caught the sound of someone crying. The wind still drowned it, but now and again it came once more. Then here, suddenly, was Nadine, sitting on a stone beside the road, wet, beaten by the wind and rain, quite unable to go another step farther, sitting there waiting — for what?

Mother was out of the car first and picked her up. "I knew someone would come, I thought it might be Rob," Nadine sobbed. Then, looking through the dark she added, "Why it is Rob, and here's Dick and Roddy. You all came!" She nestled into Mrs. Milton's arms, her sobs stopped; she was only cold and dripping and worn out.

There were the picnic blankets in the back of the car. Dick got them out and they wrapped, first Nadine, then Roddy, then each of the other boys. Mother threw a shawl around her shoulders; she was almost as wet as the others. They got in, Nadine still in Mother's arms. Rob Dale drove like a demon, but a demon in whom they all had perfect trust. The poor old station wagon groaned and cried aloud as he whirled it around turns on two wheels and put it up the steep slopes. But they were there, in almost no time at all, drawing up in front of Nadine's house where a single light still showed that not quite everyone had gone to bed.

Nadine's mother had learned, as country women do, that there is no service so great, in a moment of trouble, as to seem, at least, to know exactly what to do. She carried her little daughter up to bed, giving directions over her shoulder to her two tall daughters.

"Elaine, get one of your warm dresses out for Mrs. Milton. Edith, go into the storeroom and open that chest where Chester left his old clothes when he went away to the army. There are some there he had years ago that the boys can put on, and that last suit that was new when he went away is nearly big enough for Rob. Can you boys build up the fire? Edith, get a bowl of soup hot for Nadine and make Mrs. Milton some tea right away."

Just as she disappeared into the bedroom, Nadine called back from her mother's arms. "It was because it was your birthday, Edith, that I just had to come home."

The two pretty girls dashed here and there, brought Mrs. Milton into their room, vied with each other to offer her clothes, ran off to empty the storage chest of their older brother's garments, and brought them out, smelling heavily of camphor. They were too small for long, lank Rob Dale, a world too big for Dick and ridiculous on Roddy. But they at least were dry and warm and made it possible to spread out all their own soaked clothes to be hung up by the fire. The neat kitchen soon looked as though a whirlwind had been through it when the boys had finished dressing and hung their wet coats and trousers on chairs around the stove. But this did not seem to disturb Mrs. Wilmer who went back and forth to get things for Nadine.

"She's going to be all right," she insisted cheerfully. "The woods sheltered her when she went up the path so she was only out in the full storm for a little

THE BLUE HERON 115

while. But it was bad for her, poor little thing, when she got to the Dale house and no one was there. Rob's always been good to her, he likes children, especially Nadine. Don't you worry, Mrs. Milton, Vermont children are sturdy. But what would have happened if you had not come to find her — ?" She did not finish for her cheery voice suddenly choked.

"We can only thank God that we did find her," Mother said. "It was Anne who guessed where she had gone. And it was Rob who got us out of the water and up the hill."

The girls presently had hot supper on the table and a tray was carried in to Nadine, sitting up in bed and wrapped in blankets. It was hard to believe, but it did seem as though her adventure had done her very little harm. As for Roddy, eating smoking eggs and bacon at the kitchen table, his wild dip into the roaring waters of Stony Brook seemed to have affected him not at all. Mrs. Wilmer had said no word concerning Nadine's Aunt Cora. It was Mother who, though not mentioning her name, brought their thoughts back to how badly Nadine had fared in her house.

"The school year hasn't much further to go, only two months," Mother said to Mrs. Wilmer. "Nadine can stay with us until the term is out, and we can make sure about her visits home, that she seems to need so much. My little girls will love it."

Mrs. Wilmer did not share any of Aunt Cora's unwillingness to be indebted to the Milton family. "It would be wonderfully good of you to have her," she agreed with delight. "And I can't think she would be much trouble. I know she would be happy with you, as she hasn't been with her Aunt Cora. As I told you once, my sister, Mrs. Usher, would be glad to have her and would have been good to her, but their place is too far away."

Dick saw Rob Dale look curiously at Mrs. Wilmer as she spoke of her sister. Had he, too, noticed something out of the way about Mrs. Usher, just as Dick had? He sometimes helped at the Usher farm; Dick had seen him there once or twice. And Dick was equally puzzled about Rob himself, especially when he had seen him pick Nadine up to lift her out of the car. He remembered what Mother had said the first time Dick told her of Rob and the terrible words he had spoken in that desperate moment in the school room. Mother's first thought had been, "Perhaps he is a boy who never had a chance."

It was well after midnight when they had finished supper and Mother said, if they could, they would sleep a little before they started back. They would have to go a long way around, by a higher road, to get safely to Jefferson. "And I still wonder how you can cross the brook to get back to your house," she said to Rob Dale.

"Oh, there's a narrow place, higher up the stream," Rob told her, "where a tree blew down that I have often gone across on. It may have been swept away by now, but there's probably others that have fallen. Don't worry about me, I'll surely make it." He would not wait, he was sure that his mother would be anxious and, since his clothes were dried, he could set off at once. He almost ran out of the door, he seemed so afraid that someone might thank him or praise him.

Quiet settled down on the little house. Nadine was long since asleep. The girls wanted to give up their beds to the visitors, but Mother would not let them. She had a nap in the big rocking chair and the boys slept on blankets and pillows laid on the floor. Two hours was all that they could allow, for everyone in the village would be anxious and looking for Nadine. It was still pitch dark when they got up, buttoned up their coats, well dry now, and made ready to set off again. Only Mrs. Wilmer was awake to see them go.

Mother was drinking the cup of hot coffee Mrs. Wilmer had made for her, and was telling Roddy to hurry with his cocoa. "Did Rob tell you just how we were to go?" she asked Dick. "If it is clear to you I won't try to remember."

"I understand just how we find the whole way," Dick assured her. "There's only one bridge to cross, at the foot of the long hill that goes down west of Townsend Corners."

"It's rough while you are still this high on the mountain," Nadine's mother said. "But after you get even a little lower it is good enough going. But it is a very long way round."

They went out into the dark, held their breath for a minute as the station wagon made its favorite pretense of not being willing to start, were relieved to hear the deep rumble when the engine caught at last and the car shook with energetic life. Mrs. Wilmer did not try to thank them. Those broken words, "if you had not come to find her — " had been all that she could muster. She waved them good-bye from the door as they moved off into the dark.

It was a long way indeed, round endless curves, up and down dips and ravines, through woods and past lonely cleared farms and pastures. The blackness turned to faint gray, the shapes of the mountains began to show, and the white loops of the road before them.

Mother said to Dick as they moved steadily along, "I don't know just what to make of your Rob Dale, do you?"

"No," Dick answered frankly. "I don't know at all. I thought that he was the most surly, disagreeable boy in the whole school, and look what he did tonight."

"Once I saw him in the village," Mother said, "and he had two little girls with him. One was his sister, I think, and the other was a little mountain girl with such a pale, anxious face and a shabby dress and her hair pulled back in such a tight braid that it looked as though it must hurt. I saw Rob put her on the horse outside the ten-cent store and drop the money in to make it gallop. You should have seen her, how her face got pink and her hair came loose and blew out in curls and how she laughed out loud and was like a different child. And Rob stood there looking so pleased. He took the pair of them into the store and when they came out the girls had ice cream cones, but I noticed he didn't have any." Dick thought about that for some minutes.

"I just don't understand him," he said. "And at school he always knows all the lessons, and hardly ever talks to anybody." He gave it up.

They pressed steadily on in the darkness, mile after silent mile. "Mother must be dreadfully tired," Dick thought. "I wish I could drive."

At last there was a moment when their headlights, instead of shining on the ruts and stones before them, suddenly reached out into empty space and seemed to be trying to light the sky. The road began to go down, the headlights dipped too and they could make out that they were at the top of a very long, steep hill. Below was the level valley where the bridge should be. Mrs. Milton stopped the car.

"I'm going to wait here until daylight," she said. "I don't seem to trust bridges any too much just now. Perhaps you can get a little sleep, Dick."

Roddy had long ago curled himself up in a blanket on the back seat and was sound asleep. But Dick, sitting by his mother, was wide awake and shook his head. "I don't feel like it," he returned. And after a little pause he added, "Mother, I've been thinking about — June."

"Yes," she nodded. "So have I. June will be the end, or the beginning of our being a real part of Jefferson Village. If we don't find out what we need to know, we must give Jerry the house — in June. I cannot see any other way that would be fair."

"But there is an answer, somewhere," Dick said desperately. "I keep thinking about the person who knows it, who goes up and down, sees us, talks to us perhaps, and still doesn't tell us what we need so much to know. But how do we find that person? What more is there that we can do?"

"It seems to me we have examined every piece of paper in the house," Mother said. "Mr. Styles has gone over the accounts at the bank. Your grandfather had some dealings through New York agents, but we do not know the names of all of them. We've tried, the way Martha Jenkins said, 'to do the right thing in our own way.' The whole village has awaited for us, has stood off from us until we found the proper way. Perhaps if they hadn't held off the way they did, we never could have thought this out, or decided what we had to do. Some people have come to be friends with us in spite of themselves. I think, just the way Mr. Styles said, they would have liked to help us. All but one," she suddenly ended desperately, "all but that one person, who knows what happened and does not tell us. For I think like you, there must have been somebody, one person at least, who knows the truth."

"I think we'll know," Dick insisted stoutly. "I still think we'll find him somehow."

"And when we do," Mother spoke as though she believed in Dick's hopefulness, "when we do, all the doubts and wonderings we have had, all the things that we thought people were saying about us, will just fly away and disappear, the way the wild geese flew away when little Betsey Usher flapped her apron at them."

Roddy stirred in the back seat and half woke up. "What are we stopping for?" he asked drowsily. "Have we got home?"

"No," Mother told him. "We are waiting for day-light, and I think we can call it daylight now."

The light behind the mountains was clear and trans-parent white, with no sign yet of gold or crimson. But they could see the river winding below them, and the dark line of the bridge going over it. Certainly from above it looked high and strong and solid. Mother re-leased the brakes and the car moved quietly down the steep road. But halfway down she stopped again, glanced back at Roddy sound asleep behind them, then over at the sky above the mountains, glowing now with the orange gold light of a fair morning. She had one more thing to say, and now, it seemed was the latest moment that she could say it.

"Dick," she began, "your father has been writing and I have been wondering — whether you are happy enough here in Jefferson. Roddy has his printing and doesn't think of much else, the girls are too little to notice. But for you it is very hard, with so much anxiety, with so few friends. Would you like it if we could arrange to have you go away somewhere, back to your old school even, where they liked you so much they would be glad to take you, just for these last two months of the school year? I can't help knowing that things are hard for you here."

"And you, Mother?" Dick answered.

"Yes," she said. "I find it hard sometimes, and yet I am very happy in that house, which we have all come to love. And it is my business to be here."

"I think it is my business, too," Dick said. "And I am happy, I love that house and I like to work for it. No, I couldn't go away. There are so many things that could happen in the next two months."

A great crimson arch which was the upper rim of the sun was showing beyond the dark wall of mountains before them. It was time to go on.

The bridge was quite unharmed and solid, built high and firm above the flood waters. They rolled slowly across, looking down at the furious torrent below them, where uprooted trees, muddy underbrush, beams and planks of wrecked bridges went floating by. But the rain had practically stopped and there was a wet margin along the bank at each side, showing that the water had gone down a little and that the worst of the flood was over.

The sun was really up and its beams coming in long level light as they came along the road that brought them into Jefferson. The houses were all closed and sleeping, for everyone had been up late and even this energetic village-full was not yet up and about. But there was pale light showing in the window of Mr. Harris's house, so that Mother stopped and sent Dick to ring at the door. Mr. Harris, with two others of the selectmen behind him, came to open it.

"Now thank God for that," he exclaimed when Dick gave him their news that Nadine was found and safe.

All three of the men came out to the car. "We were waiting until six o'clock, and if she wasn't found then we were going to ring the fire bells and get everyone out to go searching through the fields and the swamps in case she had wandered off the road somewhere in the dark. You'll stop at Cora Markley's house as you go by, won't you? The poor woman has been here three times in the night to see if we had any report."

Cora Markley did indeed look like the wreck of the easy, satisfied woman who had been so unwilling to accept favors from the Milton family. "There's never been such a night in my life before," she said, standing at the car door, for she had come running out the moment she saw them stop. "And you say she's really safe?"

"Quite safe and very little the worse for her soaking," Mrs. Milton said. "She will stay at home for a few days, I believe, until it is sure that there has been no harm done. I know what a night you must have spent."

"At first I kept telling myself that she was to blame," Cora Markley said, "and I thought about the scolding I would give her when she got back. But while the hours went by I began to see that she wasn't at fault, that it was my own doing all the time, from the very first. I never saw how much she counted on getting home. I thought you were just spoiling her that first time you took her up the mountain. Well, bless you, Mrs. Milton, you and your children knew more about Nadine than I did. I should have — I should have — " Her voice broke off for she was crying.

"It's all right." Mother was patting her shoulder through the window of the car. "There is no use in grieving now when she — when everyone is safe."

Mrs. Towner was waiting for them when they came into their own drive and pulled up at the garage door. "Sylvia Jones telephoned me when she saw you stop at Fred Harris's and she said the men were smiling when they went back in so she knew it was all right. The girls were as good as gold, they were both sure you would find her. I have water on for coffee and bacon hot in the oven. Well, I must get back now, it is ten years since my cat was alone all night." She kissed Mother and went hastening away.

"I really believe she feels as though she knew us now," Dick observed as they went in to breakfast.

Roddy made himself a bacon sandwich and hurr down into the basement. "It's just time for a n of the *J.J.*," he said. "There isn't any use thinking you can get any news out that people haven't already heard," he added regretfully. "Everyone here knows about a thing practically before it happens. But they don't know, yet, about our getting into the water when the Stony Brook bridge broke up. You won't tell them about it, will you, Mother, until I can get the paper out? You were the one that saw it best."

Mother shivered. The sight of three boys in the sweeping waters of Stony Brook was something she did not care to remember. "I won't talk about it to anyone," she promised Roddy.

There was no school that day; everyone was too busy

clearing up after the night of wind and high water. Dick was taking plenty of time over his breakfast but Roddy was already very busy downstairs. He stuck his head through the basement door. "I want to say torrential flood," he said, "but how do you spell it?" On being told he disappeared again.

By and by Mr. Styles came in, his thin kind face very anxious as he asked how everyone was. Mother directed him downstairs to the offices of the *Jefferson Journal* where the story of the night's adventures was just going to press. He came up again, smiling, with the first copy of the issue in his pocket. He took it out and read the report aloud. "Roddy Milton got into the water and would be there still if it hadn't been for Rob Dale," was the editor's brief statement. "Your son has the makings of a real journalist," he told Mrs. Milton. "He never wastes a word."

He was just about to leave when someone came to the door, a tall woman with a scarf over her head and a big bag of groceries in her arms. It was the same Sylvia Jones who had telephoned Mrs. Towner. "I was just passing," Mrs. Jones said with a very casual air, "and I thought I'd run in and ask how you left little Nadine. And was it true that it was your oldest girl who guessed where she had gone?"

Mother answered her questions politely and asked her to sit down but Mrs. Jones said no, she must get on with her marketing, she was just passing, that was all. Andrew Styles grinned openly and broadly when she was gone. "There are half a hundred people at least today who would like 'just to run in,' and ask the same questions. As many as that will stop me on the way to my office to find out the same things. Now I won't keep you, for you and the boys all look like people who have been up all night."

The school was closed for several days on account of the high water and the wrecked bridges, then it began again and the days moved on as they had been doing. The last of March went by. It was in the first week of April that Dick made a new friend, an unexpected one and of an unusual kind. He was glad to add to his short list of friends, but he thought, grimly, that this one would be of no help to him in what he was seeking so desperately to find.

He was apt, whenever he had time, to climb the hill and sit for a little on the grass or on one of the big stones beside the little lake. It was beautiful to see the spring coming in the valley below, as it turned from dull winter brown to the color of half a dozen growing things, with the hillsides changing to strange delicate shades of pink and deepening red where the trees were budding. Sometimes one or another of the Ushers would be there, for they loved the place as he did. Most often it was Sam, snatching a minute from his busy day; sometimes Nora or Betsey would be with him. It was Betsey who said to him,

"Have you seen the blue heron?"

No, Dick had not. He had seen small white herons in the South, he could not really imagine a blue one. "You will see him, if you watch," Sam said.

There was one morning when he woke very early, because a very small bird with a great burst of song in his throat was singing in the maple tree outside the window. As he looked at the cool peace of his pleasant room, and caught a glimpse of the wide view outside, he thought with a pang worse than any he had felt before, that all this was slipping away, every week bringing nearer the chance of their losing it. He could not possibly sleep again, yet it would be some hours still before he must be in school. He got up, dressed and went carefully down the stairs to the kitchen.

A minute later Mother came in, soft-stepping and her eyes looking heavy as though she too had been long awake. She helped him prepare himself some breakfast and sat at the table opposite him with her cup of coffee. "I'm going out for a while," Dick told her. "I'll be back in plenty of time for school."

He laced up his heavy boots, for the woods would be dripping wet; he opened the door into the cool morning and was off up the hill. He had not thought that he would go as high as the lake, but the way seemed shorter now that he had taken it so many times, and he was out on the pasture almost before he knew it and striding across the new grass. As he came up the highest slope he thought he saw something that he did not recognize, there at the far edge of the pond. He came close very carefully, taking shelter behind the cedar trees and peering intently at the glittering water.

For a moment he thought he had been mistaken, then he knew that he had not. As his eyes got used to

the light on the ripples he could see something tall, blue-gray and thin, standing in the water, motionless because it had spied him. It was a big bird, the biggest he had ever seen, with long legs and a long beak which it was holding straight up into the morning light. It did not move as the minutes passed; its reflection in the rippling water moved more than the real bird itself. At length, however, it seemed to decide that this fellow there under the tree was not an enemy, it took a step forward, dropped its beak, made a scoop into the water, then lifted its beak again. A fish had gone down. A deep-voiced bullfrog at the other end of the pond gave a sudden, heavy swallow of sound, "Per-dunk, per-dunk."

Even that small noise and a sharper breath of wind that rustled the far bushes startled the heron, so that it spread its wings, wider than a man's arms, and flew low over the water, its legs trailing, its beautiful gray breast and its blue-washed head and neck showing their magnificent curves. It circled the pond once, then, seeming to be reasonably reassured, it settled down again to watch for fish. It was used to seeing the Ushers there; it seemed to have decided that Dick was one of their same sort.

Dick climbed the hill again and again in the next weeks, just to see the great bird more often and to take delight in its growing more and more used to his presence. Once, at the edge of the wood, he came across a tiny spotted fawn, almost invisible among the dead leaves of last year, lying absolutely still as its mother had taught it to do, while the mother herself, out of sight behind the bushes, stamped and snorted in anxiety until he went on and she could lead her child away. He saw a splendid cock pheasant, strutting and clucking, go across the path before him, he saw a bright orange oriole bringing a long trailing bit of vine to weave into her hanging nest.

There was one Saturday that dawned clear but with the air heavy, as though there might be rain later. Even this did not hold Dick back; he must have been having troubled dreams since he had awakened restless and uneasy. Not even Mother was awake as he stole about the kitchen, getting himself bacon and eggs and milk. The woods were very wet and silent, there was a heavy blanket of shining dew on the pasture grass. It almost looked as though there were marks of footsteps on the delicate surface that glittered on every hand. But even as he stopped to look they began to fade and disappear, for the long beams of sunlight were already carrying the dew away. He came to the edge of the lake and sat down on his familiar stone. The bird was not there yet, but Dick was confident that it would come. Presently it was in sight, wide-winged and dark against a rolling cloud that was coming up to cover the sun. It circled slowly, dropping down toward the pond, quite willing to light even though there was a human being there, dipping its trailing feet, closing its broad blue and gray wings, poising itself for the first stroke of its great bill at a darting fish.

It was then that Dick knew, all at once, that he and

the trusting bird were not alone, that there was the ghost of a rustle among the close-growing bushes. As he looked closer he could see that there was surely some-one there, lying along the ground, squinting down the dark barrel of a gun that was aimed at the blue heron.

CHAPTER EIGHT

"Ask There"

Although Dick had no idea who it could be who was lying there among the bushes, leveling a gun at the big bird fishing in the pond, he did not stop to look or think. He rushed upon him, threw himself forward to catch at the arm that was aiming the long barrel. Its owner tried to snatch it away and in the struggle the gun went off with what seemed like a deafening roar; the charge of shot could be heard spattering all about them among the trees and on the water, but it did not strike the heron. With a startled "Clank," that sounded more indignant than frightened, the great bird rose with a furious beating of wings and towered high above them, to go winging off to some wilder and safer region elsewhere.

"He'll never come back," Dick cried out furiously. It was only then that he had taken time to look and to see who this sudden enemy could be. The young hunter had risen to his feet and stood tall and ungainly before him. It was Rob Dale.

The bitter words which had sprung up within Dick died suddenly. The last time that a word had passed between them was on that night which Dick could never forget, when Roddy was being swept downstream in the cold stormy waters of Stony Brook and Rob Dale had cried out boldly, "I've got him." They had seen each other at the school entrance now and again and Dick had returned the quick nod which was all that Rob Dale ever gave him. But not a word had been spoken by either of them in all these weeks.

There seemed to be no words available now, but Dick knew that something must be said. He looked down at the gun lying on the grass between them and said, "I've seen that before. It belongs to Mr. Harris."

During those brief days when his father had been in Jefferson they had gone together on an errand to Mr. Harris's store and James Milton had spoken of the gun hanging on the wall, recognizing that it was something special in the way of guns. Mr. Harris had been glad to have someone with expert knowledge admire his property, he had taken it down with pride and showed them the inlaid stock, the oiled and polished fittings,

and the balance of it. Dick did not very well follow the talk since he did not know a great deal about guns. But he knew one thing.

"Aren't you under age to be using firearms?" he asked Rob. "Especially firearms that aren't yours?"

Rob Dale's thin face flushed. "No, it isn't mine but I — I borrowed it. Mr. Harris would have been willing if he had known."

"I don't believe you," Dick said angrily. "And what made you want to kill our bird, anyway? The Ushers like him, just the way I do." He remembered now that he and Sam Usher had been talking of the heron one day on the school steps, and Rob Dale had walked by. This was how he came to hear of the bird, evidently.

"I could have got good money for him, and you've done me out of it," Rob said, full of resentment in his turn. "There's a fellow up at Champlain City that stuffs and sells critters like that. I took him two foxes and a bobcat already. He promised me something extra special if I could get the big bird. Well, what are you going to do about it?" he asked at last defiantly. "Are you going to report me to the game warden?"

"I don't know," Dick's voice was hesitating and miserable. "Go on and take the gun to Mr. Harris's place. It's so early still he may not have seen that it was gone. And about the game warden — I'll have to think. I don't know what to do." He still had the picture in his mind of Roddy's white face in the swirling water and Rob's high call, "I've got him." No, he could not think what to do.

Rob Dale stood for a second seeming about to say something more, then shook his head and walked away across the hill. The sun was still so low that his shadow was long and awkward like himself as he strode away. Dick sat down on a stone, trying to think but nothing was clear. His mother had said, "What do you make of Rob Dale?" He was further than ever from being able to understand him at all. "And the heron will never come back," was still his main thought. He could not have told anybody what such a loss meant to him. The bullfrog, who seemed quite undisturbed by all that had been going on, echoed his dismal thought by one of his deep "per-dunks."

Feet were coming up the slope from the direction of the Ushers' house, and presently Sam came over the shoulder of the hill. "We thought we heard a shot," Sam said, then, sheltering his eyes with his hand against the sun, he looked after the disappearing figure going down through the pasture. "Rob Dale?" he asked, and Dick nodded.

As Sam stood there with the early sun on his face, Dick was thinking how different he was from the other boy, now gone out of sight beyond the pasture fence. Sam was square and a little stocky, but already taller than his father. In his honest blue eyes, there was quick intelligence, and, above all, a warm confident look that seemed to stand for thinking good things of everyone. His usual cheery smile was not visible now, however, for one glance at Dick's troubled face had told clearly what a question stood dark in Dick's mind. Could Sam, good friend as he was, be able to help? Sam sat down on the grass beside him.

"It's hard for anyone to make Rob Dale out," he said. "You know how smart he is. Many times I've heard the teachers and the Principal say he has much the best mind in the whole school. And he works — you know how he is about getting his lessons done. And he lives in that miserable house up on the mountain and walks down through rain and snow and mud. Did you ever know him to miss a day? I never have."

Dick sat silent. It was plain that Sam knew exactly how hard a moment this was, how impossible to decide what to do. To report to the game warden and so keep the great rare bird safe? To tell Mr. Harris, and so keep Rob from going on to get himself into even deeper trouble, but to lose his job? Sam was not trying to tell him what to decide.

"Rob's father has been dead a long time, my mother tells me. He was smart, too, and wanted Rob to have schooling, but now it's a scramble for Rob and his mother and his little sister just to get by. Every year his mother keeps saying that he will have to leave school and go to work because it gets harder and harder for them to live. Even now, you know, maybe, that Rob helps at Stone's garage Saturdays and Sunday mornings, and that he does errands and odd jobs for Mr. Harris through the week. He just can't help his mother more, and stay in school. And he wants to go on, even after high school. He told me, just once, that he didn't want to spend his life twisting bolts and greasing transmissions. He feels, I know, that he's got more in him than to do only that. But he's so desperate for money that he gets things — twisted."

Yes, that was it. Rob Dale had got things badly confused in his mind, and who could wonder. Mother had said, right at the very first, "What chance has he had?" None, compared with the chances Dick had before him. Very little even compared with Sam. Dick asked a sudden question.

"What do you want to be, Sam?"

"Me? Oh I want to be a farmer, a good farmer, that knows how and why and the real truth about how things grow and why they fail or prosper. I want to go to agricultural college, but I haven't a great deal more real hope of it than Rob Dale has. My father says he will help me any way he can, but he and I both know that isn't very much. I — I want to own this farm some day; we all love this place. I want to buy more land and plant trees on the ledge where you can't plough and — and . . ." he stopped, the sudden question had carried him away. "I talk like this and all the time we can't even pay our rent. No matter how good your mother is about it, it — it hurts. No, I'm not really much better off than Rob Dale, but I try — hard — to see things straight."

It was the first time Dick had ever seen him when he was not cheerful. The change had been very sudden, and it passed quickly. "Even if it is still early, there's a lot to do," he ended, getting up from the grass. They walked together down toward the Ushers' house. It seemed to Dick suddenly that he and Sam Usher were closer at that minute than they ever had been before, that they understood each other, that they liked the same things, that Sam knew exactly what the beauty of the mountain, the beauty of the wild things on the lake, meant to him. Here was a true and real friend. Even to have one such friend went very far.

They came to the corner of the barnyard fence and Sam stopped. They were by the well with its rough board cover and its round beam for winding up the rope that raised the bucket.

"Would you like a drink?" he asked. Dick was thirsty after his long climb and said he would. A board moved under Sam's foot as he began letting down the bucket. "I must ask Dad to fix it," he said. Things were worn and shabby on the farm but not many of them were out of order. Dick noticed that the hinge on the gate had been mended.

The bucket came up, cold and dripping, and Sam dipped a cupful for Dick. "We mostly use the deeper well up by the house," he said. "But this one has good water."

Sam's mother had been feeding the chickens and came up from the hen house with Betsey running and chattering beside her. Mrs. Usher gave Dick a quick greeting, with the odd look he had so often seen on her face, one that he could never understand. Then she hurried into the house. In his new feeling of being such real friends with Sam, Dick was sure that he could ask him anything.

"Do you think that your mother doesn't like us to come here?" he said.

Sam answered quickly, he was not trying to hide anything out of politeness. "She does like you to come, she likes it that all of you are friends with us and take the trouble to come up here." He hesitated, as though he might have gone on, but he didn't.

When you can't understand a thing it is just as well to stop talking about it, at least so Dick felt. He went off whistling down the road, thinking how beautiful the heron was and how it made up for a dozen less pleasant things that there were to think about.

Dick got home and went at once up to his room, but as he did so there was a sound of car wheels on the drive. He turned to go down just as Mother came in from the kitchen. Roddy was standing with his back against the closed front door. He had taken a glance from an upper window and he said now:

"Mother, it's Mrs. Malvern. I won't let her come in."

"Roddy," whispered Mother, "what can you mean? Of course you will." There was a thump on the knocker.

"I can't," said Roddy desperately. "I just can't." He backed closer against the door and stood staring at them both. The knocker sounded again.

Roddy looked as though nothing in a hundred years would budge him, but Mother was someone not to be disobeyed. "Just go down into the basement and you needn't see her," she whispered. "I know you don't want her to come in, and," she dropped her voice still more, "neither do I. But it will be all right."

Roddy very reluctantly removed himself from his place, crossed the hall and opened the door to the basement. He stood a moment on the top step with Dick beside him. They heard Mother opening the front door. They knew that it was not quite her natural voice which was saying, "Good morning, Mrs. Malvern. Will you come in?"

"Yes, thank you," Mrs. Malvern returned. "I came on business. They told me in the village I could get what I was looking for here. I really came to speak to your son called Roddy."

Dick and Roddy gave each other a terrified look and fled down the stairs. But Mrs. Malvern's business was certainly with them, for a moment later she and Mother were coming down too. The two boys were very busy sorting stacks of paper when the visitor got to the foot of the steps.

Mrs. Malvern was not at all like what she had been earlier. She wore a leather jacket and no hat, and she must have driven herself, for the shiny red car outside was small and there was no Phillips. She had real business with Roddy, business that was surprising in every way. They had heard in the village that she could sometimes be kind in a certain grand manner and it seemed that this was now one of those times.

"A great many people lost badly in the high water; you still hear about it everywhere. The village is getting up a big lawn supper to raise money for some of the families that were hardest hit, lost their clothes and their pigs and their chickens. Luckily there were no houses washed away. So I said they could have the lawn party out at my house, there is more space there and a bigger kitchen. I want to get three hundred supper tickets printed, just as soon as possible, so they can go right on sale. Somebody told me that one of these boys did some kind of printing."

Roddy gave a gulp, when he heard the number three hundred and looked anxiously across at Dick, but his brother was not going to let himself be frightened any more by Mrs. Malvern. "Yes, we can do it," Dick said. "My brother is the real printer, but I help him."

"He looks pretty little," Mrs. Malvern said doubtfully, but Mother joined in and told her that Roddy printed a newspaper every week and had never missed it or been late. "And he has printed tickets before," Mother said. "I think the young man who taught you how to run the printing press left you a thousand blank ones, didn't he?"

Mrs. Malvern was very particular as to how the work was to be done, although since all that the tickets had to have printed on them was "Admit One. Malvern Hill, May 15th, One dollar," it did not seem that there was much chance to get it wrong. She waited while they set up the type, and printed a sample one for her. While they were working at it she took up one of Roddy's last week's newspapers.

"Why, this isn't bad," she said. "Do you mean to say this was your own idea and you did this yourself?"

"Yes," Roddy said stiffly. "Only like we told you, Dick helps me."

She was reading the number that told about the night of the great rain. "Nadine Wilmer was lost," Roddy had related, "but got found again halfway up to her house."

"I think," said Mrs. Malvern, "I — I'd like to subscribe to it. How much is it?"

"You can see," Roddy said. "It says, 'Price — free.' "

"But why do you offer it for nothing?" she asked, more and more interested.

"Because I'm sure no one would pay me anything for it," Roddy returned, and she laughed. She looked at the sample ticket, said it would be all right, and she must have them just as soon as possible, and arranged for a price. Mother set the price — three dollars and a half. Roddy was apt to say fifty cents, when anyone asked him how much a job would be.

Mrs. Malvern walked away toward the stairs but stopped for a word to Mother before she really went away. "You own that farm up on the mountainside, don't you, Mrs. Milton?" she said. "The one where the Ushers live? My advice to you is to put the Ushers off and sell it. I've always been certain they would not be profitable tenants. I gave your father the same advice; I'm not one to keep ideas to myself, when I know they are sound. I met him in the postoffice not so many days before he died. I said to him what I have said to you, that he ought to send the Ushers away and sell the land. When I looked around I saw that the Usher woman was standing there by the mail window; she must have heard, but I am glad she did. It was high time she faced the truth about how badly things were going."

She did not seem to notice that Mother did not even try to answer her. But Mrs. Malvern looked back over her shoulder at the boys. "Now mind," she said, "I really want to subscribe to your paper. You would have to deliver it to the postoffice and put it in my box. That would be worth something, shall we say two dollars for a year? Put me down then, for a year of the *Jefferson Journal*." A year, Dick thought! And so lately she had been talking about how soon they would be going away. But this was different. This was when Mrs. Malvern wanted something.

Dick saw that the same question had struck Roddy, he saw him opening his mouth to say, "Why, you wanted us to leave!" and he could see that Mother was holding her breath for fear one of them would say it. But Mother need not have been frightened. Her two sons had better manners than Mrs. Malvern, and their visitor went out safely and without another word spoken. Mother went up the stairs with her and saw her out. She came down again as the car drove away. "I'm proud of you two," she said. "I'm going to bake you a chocolate cake."

They worked for a long afternoon. Mrs. Malvern's chauffeur, Phillips, came down, sent to see how the tickets were getting on. He stayed to help, and worked the slow, creaking old press when their arms got tired. They ate cake and he told them stories of the long motor trips over the mountains and the desert when he had taken Mrs. Malvern and her big car across the country. "She's not afraid of anything," he said, after he had told of going down a mountainside in a cloudburst of rain. "Yes, and it's right what people say, she can be kind. She just speaks too quick. And she's lonely — with all that money!" He only spoke once about the affair of the sign. "You didn't lose anything on that minnow deal." he observed. "The fishing season was about over."

Phillips carried out the finished tickets at the end of the day. He was to leave them at the postoffice and the drug store where they would be sold. Mother kept five of them and gave him the first five dollar bill for the lawn party.

"We're expecting a big crowd," Phillips said as he went away.

Talk ran quickly through the town about the lawn supper and what a large and splendid affair it was going to be. The *Jefferson Journal* had a notice of it and how everyone was getting ready to help.

"It's the kind of thing Maria Malvern likes to do," Mr. Styles said to Dick when they met one morning and walked together toward Dick's school. Dick had a sudden desperate wish to tell Andrew Styles about Rob Dale and the affair of the gun and the heron, but it was not his secret and he could not. He had made no move to report Rob to the game warden, he could not do that either. Now and then, at school, he began to see Rob give him an anxious glance, and quickly turn his eyes away. "I ought to let him know for sure what I am going to do," he thought several times. But he did not know himself.

Perhaps it was to give himself something more cheerful to think about that he began letting his mind run upon a project that was growing up in his mind. Dick did not have quite so many projects as Roddy, but they were often rather better thought out. "Mother," he said one day, "do you remember that year Dad was lecturing at the University of Minnesota and we all went up to spend the summer in the North Woods, beside a big lake, where there was an Indian reservation?"

"Yes," Mrs. Milton answered. "I remember. What put that into your head, all of a sudden?"

"Do you remember too," Dick persisted, "how the Indians used to paddle along the lake in their canoes and bend down those long stems of feathery grass that grew at the edge of the water, and shake the seeds out of the heads? They would fill their canoes up with the grains and carry them home, to sell, I suppose. And before we left in the autumn I saw ducks on their way south lighting to feed on it. What was that grass, Mother?"

It was wild rice, his mother told him. "I remember how tall and delicate and graceful it was, bending in the wind. And I do remember how the ducks settled down to eat it. Why were you thinking about it now, Dick?"

"I was thinking that it might grow up there on the little lake at the top of the hill, and the ducks would come to feed on it. Do you think we might plant some there?"

"If it grew in Minnesota, I should think it would not be too cold for it in Vermont," Mother agreed. "It is a good idea, Dick. Do you think you would have time to plant it? You're getting to be pretty busy in school now that you are getting near the end."

"I'll find time," Dick declared, and Mother, forthwith wrote to a seed company to have some sent.

It came in a big bag, one that Dick could hardly carry. Mother took him up the hill in the station wagon that afternoon. It was the last day of April. It had been warm and cold and warm again, as April weather tends to be. And today, after a morning of bright sun, clouds were suddenly coming up. Mother had some errands that could not be put off, so she left him at the end of the track across the pasture, and he climbed the last few yards with the bag over his shoulder. He had consulted Sam Usher as to whether they would mind his trying such an experiment, for was not the pond the young Ushers' Very Own Place too? Sam was helping his father today and Nora must have been in the village, for no one came out to help him. He was a little out of breath when he got up to the edge of the water and gladly swung down the bag to rest upon a stone.

Planting often sounds very easy and then turns out harder and longer than it has looked to be. One end of the small lake was rocky, with a bit of gravelly beach. It was there that the geese had attacked the little fox before Betsey Usher drove them away. But at the other end the water spread out, shallow, making pools and soft places. Here was a fine spot to scatter the rice. Dick began tossing it out in handfuls, bigger and bigger ones as he went on, spreading it evenly, finding what a large stretch of ground it would be possible to cover. He was thinking of the wild ducks coming down, reaching to right and left, quacking and gobbling as they found the new food.

He was soon hot and weary, and also very dirty, for the rice was dusty and got into his hair and down his collar. But he would not stop until it was all spread and the bag was empty. He sat down then, and mopped his dusty face, and leaned back against a cedar tree. How tired he was. And it was beginning to rain.

An April storm had blown up, in a very black cloud that came sweeping and trailing its shadow across the wide valley. The rain came down in a sheet, shutting out the wide view. Dick buttoned his coat, beginning to wish that he had brought his sweater. He wrapped the empty seed bag around his shoulders.

Someone, to his surprise, was coming out from the shelter of the woods below and striding across the bare pasture. On account of the wind, this boy's head was bent low, or was it a man? It was blowing so hard Dick could not tell. The rain came down more furiously, there was a queer roaring in the air and suddenly it had begun to hail; round glittering flecks of ice were falling upon the new grass, piling up under the bushes, growing bigger and bigger, bouncing and rattling as they fell. Dick drew in his feet and crouched close under the thick cedar branches, they must be striking hard on the head and arms of that person coming toward him. Who could it be, why didn't he turn back? Dick could hear him panting as he came across the grass, running now to get to shelter, still with his head bent. He came up the last slope, pushed forward into the shelter of the cedars and threw himself down, completely out of breath. Dick saw now that it was Rob Dale.

"I was down at your house," Rob said, "and your mother said you were up here. I had to find you."

Dick unwrapped the seed bag and spread it over the knees of both of them, to keep out some of the rain. He could not imagine why Rob wanted to speak to him, and he did not ask. He could not be looking for the heron again, the boy thought bitterly. He had seen nothing of the great bird since that miserable morning.

"There was something I had to ask you," Rob was saying, not finding it easy to speak but pushing on just the same. "I have to know whether you — whether you have spoken to Mr. Harris — or to the game warden about the gun — and the bird."

"I haven't," Dick told him. He knew now that at last he had made up his mind. "And I'm not going to."

Rob Dale drew a long breath and let it out slowly. It must have been hard to wait and not know. Particularly hard, and now Rob was explaining why.

"There's to be a new filling station opening next

month. Duke Klein is running it and he offered me a job for the summer, better than anything I've had before. But he said I had to get a recommendation from the man I had been working for — that would be Mr. Harris. He would have to say that he would stand back of me."

"And you can't ask him to recommend you until you know what I said to him?" Dick asked.

Rob did not speak for a minute. "I know what you were thinking that day about seeing me in the schoolroom when I was looking at Miss Evans's watch. I know you won't believe me; you needn't; but the mortal truth is that I was just standing there thinking what it would be to me, if that watch was mine and I could turn it into money, money for my mother and for making it so I could stay in school longer, a whole year more of school."

Dick nodded. "Sam Usher told me — that it was hard for you, how much you needed something to go on. Yes, I — I think I believe you. Anyhow it doesn't matter now."

"But it matters what you think, what Mr. Harris would think if he knew about the gun. I got it put back before he ever saw it was gone. And it's the mortal truth, too, that I was only borrowing it."

"But could you ask him, about a recommendation, when he didn't know that you took it?" Dick asked. There was a long pause. "I thought I could," Rob said. "I told myself if only you were not going to say anything, I could ask him. But — but, I reckon after all I can't. I get things twisted, sometimes, when I think so hard about what I need, what I want, how I feel I could be something, if only there was a chance to learn."

There was silence between the boys again, until at last Dick said, "You could tell him you borrowed the gun. Then you could ask him." "And what chance would there be then that he would give me a recommendation?" Rob asked bitterly. "There's no one thinks too much of me even now. Abner Harris told me once I was getting to think crooked."

"But he wants you to think straight," Dick insisted. "He was telling my mother what a good worker you are. And she was telling him how you pulled Roddy out of the water. Try it," he urged, and when the boy beside him did not answer he said again, "Try it."

The rain had swept by, the sharp rattle of the hail had stopped. The black cloud was breaking. Rob Dale got up. "I could try it," he said, then added, "no I couldn't, I couldn't. He never would." He stood thinking and his face grew firm. "I will," he ended. "I vow I will. But — without you, I wouldn't have." He took a long step away across the grass, and another, then turned back. He seemed to think that there was something that he could do for Dick in return.

"You're looking for something," he said. "You want to know the answer to a question and you haven't found it."

Dick felt his breath coming short. "You know — ?" he asked. "You know the answer?"

Rob shook his head. "I don't know the answer," he said. "But I might know who does." He looked across the shoulder of the hill toward the Usher house, where its roof showed above the edge of the slope. He jerked his head toward it. "Ask there," he said, and strode away down the pasture. The sun came out around him, glinting on the little piles of ice, still heaped all across the slope. He walked faster and faster as he went down. He was running before he got to the fence and disappeared into the woods.

CHAPTER NINE

The Lighted Window

No one could ever foresee whether Roddy was going to be the first one ready for school in the morning, or the last. Sometimes he was nearly at the end of his eggs and bacon and milk and carrying his plates into the kitchen when the others came down — that was on the days when he still had some work to do on the *Jefferson Journal*. Sometimes he came rushing down at the last second, his shoes in his hand and his shirt collar flapping and Mother had to say finally that he could not sit down to eat until he was properly dressed. But on this next morning Dick, still full of the troubles of Rob Dale, noticed vaguely that his brother was managing to be, somehow, both early and also late.

He finished breakfast before the others, and went up-stairs again, said a few impatient words to the two girls who had slipped into the guest room to look at their new checkered pink dresses in the long mirror. He came down again, stood about looking vaguely anxious and still was not ready when the others were, and so let the three of them set off without him.

"Roddy, what is it that is on your mind?" his mother asked, as she cleared the last dishes off the table with that quick neatness which was so like Mother and unlike anyone else.

"Is it wrong, Mother, if I have a secret, something I don't tell even you about, just right now?" he answered.

"No." Mother considered a little. "If it is something I wouldn't mind about."

"You wouldn't mind a bit," Roddy brightened quickly. "And couldn't you perhaps drive me to school, you see it is beginning to rain a little."

"The others didn't mind getting a trifle wet," she protested in some wonder, for usually Roddy was the last of all four of them to mind about rain. "Or," she guessed with a shrewd smile, "Are you afraid of getting the secret wet."

"That's it," her son answered immediately and much pleased. "Can we go right now?" He was upstairs in a moment and came down again with a very large paper-wrapped bundle under his arm. Mother had gone out to back out the car; he slipped into one of the rear seats, putting the bundle carefully on the floor. The school bell was just ringing and everyone had gone inside when the station wagon stopped before the school and Roddy thanked his mother, slid out quickly and ran in by the side door.

The fact that Roddy, with the help of all his family, had come to do so many of the small printing jobs of Jefferson Village, gave the Miltons the chance of knowing about most public events before they came about. They were presently all at work correcting, sorting and counting the great pile of handbills being printed for the school announcing the Spring Hobby and Pet Show, Exhibition of Handicrafts, (these being both from the School Shop and done at home,) and Distribution of Prizes.

The very last days of the school year were so full of the festivities of High School graduation that this important day for the younger students was always set earlier, for the first evening of May. It came therefore even sooner than Mrs. Malvern's Lawn Party for which tickets were selling so briskly that twice Roddy and Dick had been called on to print more of them.

Everyone knows how busy a whole school becomes as the year gets toward its end. This must be finished and that. The last books must be read and accounted for, the last pages of the arithmetic, worn and fuzzy from the toiling hours that have been spent on them, have to be turned over and put out of sight forever. The

apron that Bella was making in the sewing class was
finished and ironed. The coffee table for the porch,
which Dick and Roddy together had been making in
the school shop, got its final coat of paint. Martha
Jenkins had said, one day when she came in with wet
laundry, "It's the whole of this house your family
ought to set on show, Mrs. Milton. They've put so
much work here. I wonder they've had time for making
things at school."

The first of May came, hot, as even early spring
days sometimes are, with apple blossoms rushing out,
and clouds of cherry white beginning to blow away.
There was singing and marching at school in the
morning. Then the moment lessons were over, all
turned their hands to sweeping the big auditorium,
putting the great bunches of flowering branches all
about, setting out the baskets of flowers on the stage.
The school board would be there, and the selectmen.
"You're coming, Mother, aren't you?" all the young
Miltons asked in turn and she assured each one, "Yes,
I'm coming."

Nadine had spent these last weeks with them, but
her father and mother had come down the mountain
for this occasion. And the little girl had gone to her
aunt's to have supper with them.

The big room was over-crowded that evening and
over-lighted and breathlessly hot, when the Miltons
arrived there, all together. They had not known how
quickly it would fill up so that they had to take seats
far back, wedged into a tight row with Bella on the

end. Some people nodded to them as they came in, and stout Mrs. Evans, who filled more than a whole seat, looked down at Anne who sat next to her and said, "I'm sorry," for it was very plain that the little girl was being squeezed. A bell rang and everyone was quiet, and the ceremonies began.

Mr. Harris, looking not much like himself in a white collar and, as Roddy said, "Selectman clothes," gave a little speech about the school and how much time and thought and money the town put into it. The best thing about the speech was that it was short. The glee club sang some very pleasant songs, and the orchestra played a good bouncing march. Then the president of the school board got up to give out prizes. Rob Dale got the first one for the best grades of the year. The young physics teacher, who had taught Roddy to print, had seen to it that the book Rob won was a fat volume on mechanics and not on poetry. The best athlete of the year got a cup, and there were others.

While they were being distributed a good deal of disturbance seemed to be going on behind the big doors which made the back of the stage. Mr. Harris felt, finally, that he had to explain. The next list of prizes would be for hobbies and handicrafts, he said. And each prize exhibit would be brought out to be shown in its turn. Getting them in line back there seemed to be hard to accomplish without a good deal of noise. There was only one more of the school board's prizes to award, the one for the best record of attendance.

In deciding who was to have this, he explained, they took into account not only the fact of no days being missed, but the distance and the difficulty of the student's getting there.

It was little Nadine Wilmer to whom the prize was given. For those two days after the great storm she had stayed at home, but there was no school with the roads all running like rivers, so she had missed nothing. Mr. Beggs, the School Board President, read out her name. She got up from the row in front of the Miltons and went down the aisles to get her prize, a fine and glorified lunch box. There had been steady clapping of hands to honor each prize winner. She had more than the others as she walked up, looking small and frightened but pleased.

Two big boys had been moving a tall frame onto the stage and set it up behind Mr. Beggs while he was still talking. Dick heard Anne give a sudden little gasp of surprise, even before he recognized what they were carrying in. It was Anne's patchwork quilt, Mother's Christmas present. But how had it ever got there? Dick suddenly noticed the smooth self-satisfied grin on Roddy's face and knew who had entered it. The quilt, hung up like a picture, with its pattern of big baskets of flowers in their old, lovely, unfaded colors, was something indeed to be very proud of.

The teacher who had charge of sewing was announcing the award. For the best and most beautiful piece of handicraft done at home. Anne Milton.

Anne got up, with a little difficulty, from next to

Mrs. Evans and stood for a second. She did not go forward and with great effort she found her voice, a shy little voice, but heard by everyone, for the room was very still. "But I didn't do it all myself."

The teacher knew the answer to that. She told the little story of Anne's great grandmother and how the quilt was interrupted when it was only two-thirds completed, and lay so long with no further stitch taken.

"To finish it, to do it so well that no one can tell where one hand stopped and another began, to follow out the pattern so completely and exactly, has made it a better piece of work than if it had all of it been new. Miss Anne Milton will please come forward to receive her prize." Anne came, a little bigger than Nadine, shyer, more hesitating, not sure of herself in this crowded company where, while she knew most of the other children, scarcely one of the elders was more than an acquaintance. There had begun to be a clapping of hands, and, little by little it grew, as though an idea grew within every mind and heart in that gathering. Perhaps it was because they had seen Nadine go forward and come back that they began to remember that day of driving storm and rain, when the whole village was full of terror over news that a child was lost, and the Milton family, from whom they had all held back their approval, coming forward to the rescue. Anne had guessed where Nadine had gone. Mrs. Milton and her boys had gone in search, up roads almost impassable, over bridges so far from safe that one boy had come close to losing his life. The

clapping rose to a perfect thunder of applause as
Anne walked up the platform — feet stamped, voices
sounded, fat Mrs. Evans was wiping her eyes. Anne
looked bewildered, Bella was wildly excited but Mother
and the two boys sat looking before them, color
mounting in Mother's cheeks, Roddy laughing with
delight. His secret, that of entering Anne's quilt for
the exhibition, had indeed been nothing that Mother
would mind.

Confusion filled the rest of the evening. Pets were
being judged, dogs were yelping, a turtle and a white
rat got away, and nervous ladies were, a few of them,
inclined to climb on the seats not remembering that
the rat could climb far more nimbly than they. Then
in the end, the showing was over. People were drifting
out into the big room next door where a long table
groaned with the heartiest of refreshments. But people
were passing by the roast beef sandwiches, the baked
beans, the flaking mince pies. They were crowding
about the little island of five Miltons, shaking hands
with Anne to congratulate her, to say to Mother how
proud she must be of her children, to commend the
Jefferson Journal. More than one of the older men
showed that he had a copy in his pocket. It was
not necessary for any of the Miltons to say much, they
only needed to smile and shake another hand, and nod
acknowledgment. Dick felt his hand suddenly clasped
in the big bony grasp of Rob Dale and heard a word in
his ear. "It was all right." Mr. Styles came up.

"Everyone in Jefferson is here tonight except Maria

Malvern," he said. "I wish she had come. She would know that the Milton family is here to stay."

People scattered at last, for Jefferson went to bed early. The Miltons were glad to get into the quiet and shelter of their own house, with soft air coming in the open windows and voices saying good night to each other all down the street. Bella was drooping with sleepiness, but Dick never felt more wide awake. Mother's eyes were shining.

"They've changed their minds about us at last," Dick said and she nodded. "I never really understood before. But they were just so honest that they had to wait until they were sure."

Dick went slowly up the stairs to bed. He was relieved and happy like the others but — but — nothing was really changed. The people of Jefferson had suddenly believed in them, and knew that, as Martha had said, "they would do the right thing in their own way." But what was the right thing? Was it any clearer than it had been? May had begun, they were in their last month before June and they knew no more than they had known all along. Yes — perhaps a very little more. There had been that jerk of Rob Dale's head toward the Usher house and his brief words, "Ask there." Dick had not asked. He had not even talked to his mother yet, for he felt that it was his business, and that of no one else to "ask there." He had been waiting for the right minute to ask Sam.

It came on the afternoon when Sam offered to help him plant the vegetable and flower seeds in the garden patch behind the Devons house, which they had already dug up and made ready. Peas and radishes were already up, but the smooth mahogany-colored bean seeds were to be put in and the different varieties of corn to ripen at proper intervals in the summer. The earth was fine and black and crumbly between their fingers as they marked out the rows and dropped the seeds in place. The sun came down warm about their shoulders, falling through the branches of the maple tree. It was a good time, but Dick was fumbling for the words. There was nothing for it but to ask direct.

"You know — there's something we've been trying to find out about my grandfather and Jerry Stewart's money — "

Sam nodded, "Yes, I know."

"And do you think," Dick persisted, "that he might ever have said anything at your house, to your father or mother, about what he had done with it or meant to do with it?" It certainly was a long chance, but it was true that Dick's grandfather had been there, on the last day he went anywhere.

Sam was thinking carefully. "I remember that he came up that afternoon, it was the last time we saw him. He went up to the barn with my father to see about some repairs. I wasn't with them all the time, but certainly they didn't talk about money at all, just plans for the farm. And I heard my father say only last week when we were working in the barn that he knew what it meant to you to be in such doubt about the money, but that he had no idea."

"And — and your mother," Dick said desperately.
"Could he have said anything to her?"

"Mr. Devons hardly talked to my mother at all. I
saw her at the door of the house, but she said my father
was at the barn, so he went right up there, and afterward he and my father went down to the town together
to order lumber. Mrs. Malvern once said something to
your grandfather in the postoffice, advising him not to
rent the farm to us any more. My mother overheard
her, and I think mother was a little afraid of Mr.
Devons ever after, even though he was always so kind.
But he never told us anything."

There it was, and no person could ever disbelieve
Sam Usher. Dick bent his back to the planting; they
dropped the last seed, and went in for Mother's lemon-
ade and cookies.

Everyone now was talking about the lawn party at
Mrs. Malvern's. The school festival and prize giving
had involved only a smattering of the school and the
village, but this was something very different. People
from towns all about were coming. There was to be
music and dancing. All of the girls and many of the
older women were getting new dresses. The village
girls and the women were all going to wait on the
tables at the supper; it would make more profit for the
flood sufferers. But the supper itself would be cooked
by Mrs. Malvern's own helpers and served out of her
kitchen. Mrs. Malvern had said vaguely that perhaps a
few ladies might like to bring cake. Mother shook her
head once or twice when she heard about the plans.

"And she has gone away and won't even be back here until two days beforehand."

People kept saying to the Miltons. "Are you coming to the Lawn Party?" They had not said that before.

"I wish we could get the Ushers to come," Dick said to his mother and she answered, "I have been thinking about that too, Mrs. Usher and all. Perhaps if we asked her to bring something she might."

Nora and Sam when spoken to at school said that their mother would be glad to send a cake. "And we hope we might get her to come," Nora said. "We will let you know." But the next few days were so busy that Dick did not see the Ushers again and the great evening itself was now at hand.

On the afternoon before the party Dick stayed late at school, partly because he had work to finish, partly, really, because he was rather tired of hearing so much talk and excitement about the coming evening. He got home to find the house already in a whirlwind of preparation. Even Mother, out in the kitchen, putting a snowdrift of white cocoanut over the two big golden cakes on the kitchen table, looked flustered. The girls' freshly ironed dresses were hanging up and Roddy had been sent upstairs to get the printer's ink off his hands.

"I believe I'll just take a walk up the hill," Dick said. "There is still plenty of time to get ready. That is unless I can help you." Mother needed to be in seven places at once, but they were places where she and she alone was needed, so she shook her head. And she seemed to understand fully just how Dick felt.

"Don't make me anxious by coming back late," she said, and he went out.

It was pleasant climbing upward through the cool woods, with the evening coming on. He saw a deer crossing an open glade — perhaps the same buck he had seen on that first day of exploring. A little later he saw a doe and two fawns; this was the hour when deer liked to come out to graze. He crossed the open pasture, telling himself he ought to go back. He would only go a little farther. But the moon would be up in a few minutes. He had never seen the little lake by moonlight. And there was always a lingering hope in his mind that the blue heron might come back.

Long shadows lay across the surface of the water and lined the banks, as he came near. He stood silent beside a cedar tree looking and looking again. Was that something at the far edge of the water — something tall, unmoving, then darting suddenly into quick motion to become instantly still again. It was the heron, he could see it now, erect, its bill poised above the ripples, waiting, waiting, then striding suddenly forward to dip and lift that long beak. And once more utter stillness. Dick stood as immovable as he, beginning to think at last that the bird knew he was there, was watching, was willing again to trust a little in that human being who did not seem to be there to harm him.

The moon came up, a great pale bubble floating above the hilltop, its white light moving slowly across the water. He could see the bird clearly now, a silver

statue with its strong poised neck, its smoothly shaped body showing a faint reflection in the water. It certainly could see him there beside the tree: it must be watching him; it was not afraid. At last it moved, spread its great broad wings with their arched shoulders, mounted easily up and up, its legs trailing backward, circled over the black tree tops and was gone into the sky.

Dick swung quickly into the path that led over the slope toward the Usher house. He had certainly stayed too long; he would make better time now by joining them and going down the hill with them in their car. A cloud had come over the moon but his feet easily followed the path in the dark.

The new grass was soft under his tread as he cut off the turns in the path that went steeply down toward the house. He heard voices below and saw the moving lights of the little car coming out of the shed. Should he call to them? Probably they would not hear him above the noise of the car. Were they all going?

No, he heard voices calling good night and then a door slammed. The car moved away. There was still a light in the kitchen, a moving light. Mrs. Usher had not gone with the rest, she was going across to the steep stairs carrying a lamp. She was going up and up he noticed, beyond the room above, to the attic overhead.

Where he stood there on the steep slope was opposite the attic window and not too far away, so that he could see clearly the low rafters, the stretch of wall opposite the window, the door to the stairs, opening as

Mrs. Usher came through it. She looked back over her shoulder as though to see if, by any chance, anyone was behind her. Was she frightened, Dick wondered, should he call out to her that he was there. Something kept him silent as she came up the last step and closed the door.

She set the lamp on a shelf and opened what seemed to be the door of a little cupboard. She was taking out what looked like some papers; he thought he caught the shape of a big envelope. Dick forgot everything else as he stood and wondered. He took a step forward to see better and his foot touched a loose stone which slipped and turned over and went rolling down the hill. On the instant Mrs. Usher had blown out the light.

They both stood, two people holding their breath in the dark. There was no sound from the house, no spark of light as the door on the stairs opened again. Mrs. Usher was waiting, waiting, to make sure whether or not someone was out there, someone who had caught a glimpse of her opening the cupboard door. Dick moved one foot noiselessly on the grass and then another, stepping backward, turning cautiously, going back up the hill again, swiftly and without a sound. Rob Dale had been right indeed, someone in that house knew a secret. It must be his secret for which he had so long sought the answer. He was over the shoulder of the hill now and running with all his speed across the pasture to carry the news home.

CHAPTER TEN

Admit Five

The whole family was gathered in the hall
when Dick came rushing in from his journey up the
hill. The girls looked like little fairies, as little girls do
when they are going to a party, with their ruffled skirts
standing out around them and with flyaway hair
ribbons. Roddy looked a little quenched with his hair
so smooth and in his striped blazer, but his hands
were free of ink and his necktie was firmly straight.

"Mother's been worrying," Bella began reproach-
fully, but his mother took one glance at Dick's face
and shook her head.

"I think Dick may have his own reason," she said, as Dick went upstairs two at a time.

"Get out the car," he called over his shoulder as he ran. "I will be ready in five minutes." He was good at speedy change of clothes, and was as well and carefully dressed as any of the other Miltons when they all got into the car together. Mother was in white and looking her prettiest. Even the old station wagon had been washed.

"I want to be proud of my family," Mother said. This was the Miltons' first party in Jefferson.

They drove up the long hill and came to the big house all full of flowers and with hanging lanterns to light the lawn. Roddy handed in the five tickets, each saying Admit One. He was proud of printing them. Guests were already sitting at little tables, talking. Dick noticed at once that something was not quite right. The people at the tables sat there with empty plates that had once had chicken on them and salad, and now they were waiting. Was it for ice-cream, perhaps. But where was it?

They sat down at a table and filled all its seats, but no one brought any food. "Perhaps we have to get it ourselves," Mother said. "I'll just carry my cake in and see." She went away, going in at the kitchen door and in a minute she was out again making signs to Dick to come. When he started she beckoned again, they were all to come, all four. They were surprised but they followed Dick and went in.

Dick had never seen anything like that kitchen

before. It was big and full of shining white things —
tables, a great big stove, a bigger sink. But even more
it was full of people, all talking at once. The tables
were full of dirty dishes, girls with trays were shouting
for ice cream and bumping into each other. The cook,
standing at the stove over a great pan of chicken,
was crying. Mrs. Malvern was standing in a doorway
scolding at the top of her lungs. People were coming
in with used dishes, nothing was going out. The place
was getting fuller of noise and confusion every minute.

"Really, Mrs. Milton, do you think this is a place
to bring your children? Aren't there enough people
here already?" Mrs Malvern was saying. Her voice
was high and shrill. People stopped talking for a minute
to see what Mother would say. Mother answered
quietly. "I want people to see how the Milton family
can wash dishes. It seems to me there are a lot of dishes
here to be washed."

She stood them in a row along the sink, the Milton
production line, Dick to pile and scrape, Roddy to
wash, little Bella to rinse, Anne to wipe. The dishes
moved steadily, mother carried them away and set
them out on the long table near the door. "Now,"
she said to Phillips, who was in a big blue apron,
lifting a great can of ice-cream, "Fill them up here,
and set them on the trays." The girls who were helping
at the tables carried them away, the room cleared,
more plates moved along, the cook filled them with
chicken and peas and rolls, and they were taken away
and the room was quiet at last, with everything going

like clockwork. Mrs. Malvern stood in the doorway still, staring and with her mouth open. Nearly an hour went by. There was great chattering and laughing outside, the lawn party was being a great success.

"There now, dear, don't you and your children in their good clothes wash any more of those dishes. But it surely is a sight to see the way they do it." Mrs. Towner had come to help, she brought three women with her, and the Miltons gave up their places; their arms were beginning to ache. Mother had cut up her cake, she had cut another and another. She came close and Bella said, "I'm a little tired, Mother. Are we going to stay much longer?"

"No," said Mother, "we're going now." They slipped out. Mrs. Towner was trying to thank them, but Mother wouldn't let her. "It wasn't anything," she said. "My children are glad to help."

"We could have managed all right, where we were used to serving supper," one of Mrs. Towner's friends said. "At the church hall we can take care of fifty people at a time. But three hundred, and in Mrs. Malvern's kitchen! And," she added in a lower tone, "with Mrs. Malvern shouting at you!"

Other people tried to thank them too. Mrs. Malvern had disappeared, she was out on the lawn still receiving guests. "Yes, it seems to be going well," they heard her say to Jerry Stewart, who had just come. But the Miltons were truly tired out, they were glad to climb into the station wagon, edge their way out through all the parked cars and go away down the hill.

When they got home and came in Roddy said suddenly, "I never thought of it, but we didn't have any supper. *I'm hungry.*" It was not until Mother brought out ham and made biscuits, had whipped cream to put on gingerbread, that they began to laugh. They were still laughing when Jerry Stewart came in and he was laughing too. They gave him a rousing welcome.

"Mrs. Malvern says that everything went beautifully and that there is lots of money for the High Water Fund." he told them. "She says she is very proud over making such a success. And everyone, except perhaps Mrs. Malvern, is talking about the Milton family and how they saved the party."

Dick had hardly had more than a dozen words of private talk with his mother.

"I have something to tell you," he had said to her. "Someone does know about the money. It's Mrs. Usher." And when she exclaimed, "How could it be?" he repeated firmly, "Yes, I'm sure. Things just all seem to come together, somehow, and I know it's the answer."

Jerry Stewart was saying good night and the little girls had to be got to bed, so there was no more chance to say anything. His mother came into his room very late, with the church clock booming midnight, but she only said:

"I'm too tired to think clearly tonight. You must tell me the whole thing in the morning."

The girls hung about their mother in the morning and a man came to see about some painting. "Mr.

Harris sent me over," he explained, "Harris says those high ceilings are no fit job for a woman or boys, no matter how good they are at it."

After lunch, when Dick and Mother wiped the last of the dishes, he had a chance to tell her fully what he had seen, what he thought. "It all seemed so clear last night," he said finally, "but today it isn't quite the same. But Sam said something yesterday about how Mrs. Malvern frightened her, saying Grandfather ought to stop renting the farm to them — oh, I don't know — ." His voice trailed off. "It just came to me, and I might be wrong."

"I don't believe you're wrong," Mother answered. "We'll — no, I can't think what to do about it quite yet."

The girls went to sleep after lunch and so, at last, did Roddy, who was tired after a long morning of printing. Mrs. Towner came over and said the robins were getting their cherries and would they mind if she picked some, because they would be all stolen by the birds before tomorrow. Mother had made a great cherry pie for dessert that day. "Do take all you can," she urged Mrs. Towner, "and while you are here, Dick and I may go out for a little while." Mrs. Towner was glad to stay. "I'll sit and stone the cherries in your kitchen, so the girls won't be alone," she agreed.

"Where are we going?" Dick asked. "Are you going to speak to Mr. Styles?"

"No," Mother said. "We're going to ask Jerry Stewart now what he thinks. I must know." It was plain that Mother thought Dick's idea was something really important.

They had never been to Jerry Stewart's house before. It was at the other end of the village and stood close to the street with a fence around it, a small white house with a very big chimney in the middle. It was very old, Mother said, older than theirs, and the space inside the fence was full of flowers. They came to the door and Jerry opened it before they rang, with Chris wagging his tail in welcome behind him. The little hall inside had steep stairs going up from it, and a door stood open to show that on the left was Jerry's study. It was a long room with a big desk and straight stiff chairs, and with everything set straight and neat, "as though it was a ship's cabin," Mother said afterward. There were pictures of ships on the walls and Dick caught sight of a letter on the table addressed to "Commander Gerald Stewart." He had forgotten that their friend was a naval officer; of course no one in Jefferson called him Commander.

He moved an armchair out for Mother to sit in. There was a bowl of flowers on the table next to her, and a bowl of pipes also which he moved away. He had greeted them but he did not ask any questions. He sat down now and just waited. Mother and Dick took turns at explaining, at telling Jerry how long they had been troubled over whether he or they ought to have the house, how they had promised each other that things must be settled one way or another by June. They told him what Dick had seen and what he suddenly thought last evening, "I believe Mrs. Usher knows."

Jerry nodded now and then, he did not interrupt in the whole time — and he spoke of the last thing first. "It may indeed be possible that Sarah Usher is connected with this somehow. I have always known her well and liked her. I have thought of her as a kind, sensible woman. But some change came over her while I was away at sea so long. She is not like herself. I am sure something is troubling her very greatly, although what that can have to do with you and your children, Mrs. Milton, and with the money I gave your father to keep for me, is hard for me to see."

Then he went back to the whole beginning. "It is true, just as Andrew Styles told you, I turned over a sum of money to Roger Devons, so that he could invest it for me. I think Andrew Styles told me that you know what investing money is?"

"Yes," Dick answered, "and Mother told me some more."

"We do not just let loose dollars lie around, when we do not need them all," Jerry said, "so we put them where they will be of some use." He had known that, since he was going into the Navy, he would be away a very long time. Roger Devons was wise about money, he had always advised Jerry and his father. Jerry did not hear much from Jefferson while he was away, only at last that Roger Devons had died, after a very short illness, "and that he had left his house and the mountain land to the Miltons."

"I was sure that when I came home I would find some record of the money I had left with him," Jerry said. "And of what he had done with it. Andrew Styles had already been searching, but he could not make out what had happened. Neither could I. We did everything we could to find out. Then I told him that I would rather lose the money than bring any claim that would look as though Roger Devons had done anything amiss with it. So we let the matter rest, but of course, even though we had been careful, the whole village was whispering about it by that time."

"But you told me that first morning on the hill, that we must try to find out what had really happened," Dick said. And Jerry answered, "Yes, when I saw that it was spoiling your chance of a happy life here, I decided it was time to try again. I thought you could find out more about your grandfather's affairs than I could." He got up and walked up and down the room once or twice, before he went on.

"Of course I knew what the Jefferson people had decided, bless their kind hearts, that I ought to have the house instead of the money. What would I want with a great big house like that, particularly when it was just right for all of you. But Jefferson people would be bound to have some idea of their own about the matter, and there would be no use in arguing with them. And in spite of everything, they have not been able to hold out in keeping a welcome from you. As I have heard and seen, you and your children have more friends every day. And Roddy's newspaper is read in every house in the town."

"But now we must talk about Mrs. Usher again," Mrs. Milton said. "You say you think Dick may be right?"

"Dick says that she took alarm at what Mrs. Malvern said when she advised Mr. Devons not to rent the farm to them any more. What a woman Maria Malvern is for saying things to upset people. It's partly because she is never thinking about anyone but herself and partly because she isn't happy. Now," he ended, sitting down again and crossing his legs comfortably, "we will have to make a plan. I really believe we may be on the right path. Surely I can't have you making me a present of a house on the first of June."

They could not settle on much of a plan except that Dick and Jerry should go up to see Mrs. Usher just as soon as Jerry could make time, since he was busy now writing a naval report.

"There is no use in my going, I upset her the minute I come near," Mother said. This was true, though it was hard to believe.

"But I think," Jerry insisted, "that we really could put the whole thing right before her, Dick could tell her how troubled you have been, not knowing what Roger Devons did with my money, and we can ask her, straight, did he ever by any chance or at any time speak of it to her."

They had to leave it at that. Jerry brought them in a tray of tea and crackers with some wonderful jam that must have come from the other side of the world, and then they went home. Jerry was to be busy for the rest of the week, so that there was nothing for Dick to do but wait.

Jerry Stewart met Dick on the street on Friday evening, however, and stopped to speak to him. He would have time to go up to the Ushers' farm tomorrow morning, he said, if Dick still wanted to go. "I am not sure how much good it will do to ask Mrs. Usher any questions," he said. "But it is worth trying."

Warm midsummer air was over everything when they drove up the hill next morning, although it was still only the last of May. When they got to the Usher farm and stopped to get out near the barnyard gate, nobody was in sight. "They are probably all of them up at the strawberry patch," Jerry guessed. The door of the house stood open, but there was certainly no one inside. "Look, there is Betsey coming down the hill. Hello, Betsey," he called.

The little girl, who considered Jerry Stewart her special friend, called back to them and began to run. To make the way shorter, she came down along the barnyard fence, and ran across the wooden platform that covered the well. She stumbled in her haste and tripped over the loose board which needed to be mended. It gave way under her with a sharp crack. For an instant they saw a flash of red curls and then she had disappeared.

Dick was choked with horror, but Jerry let out a great shout:

"Help, come quickly!" Someone answered above but it sounded a long way off.

Dick and Jerry had run to the spot where Betsey had vanished; Jerry was jerking the boards away. The bucket had been drawn up and out, and was standing on the grass to dry. Jerry was cutting at the knot of the rope on the handle, then was tying the end into two big loops.

"Dick," he said. "It's got to be you to go down after Betsey. You couldn't wind up the rope to pull the two of us out, if I went down on the end of it. The pulling up is for me and no one else can get here in time. Can you do it? Will you go down?"

Dick did not even take time to answer. He was already seated in one of the loops Jerry had made and had his knees in the other. Jerry lifted him over the edge of the well curb and, unwinding the rope slowly as the round beam turned, he began to lower him downward.

CHAPTER ELEVEN

The Answer

The inside of a well is not like anything else. It is lined with stones, smooth and slippery, with moss in the cracks and little tufts of ferns. It is very cool, and very quiet, and it gets darker and darker as you go down.

"It is like a railroad tunnel," Dick thought, looking up at the round spot of light at the top, growing smaller, smaller. He had to sit very still or the rope would begin to swing and bump him against the the sides. He was not frightened, there hadn't been time to be. He just could not believe that it was really happening. Sam had said that the well was not very deep, but he seemed to be moving down a very long way. The glimmer of water at the botton grew clearer, as the light at the top went farther and farther away. There had not been a sound from Betsey.

She was standing up to her chin in water, but she was standing, her feet were on something solid. Old wells have a long history, and one of the things that happen is that careless people let the bucket come untied and it falls into the well for good. There was one old bucket in the bottom at least, and perhaps more. Betsey was standing on the heap of old rusted metal, steadying herself by a hand against the stones of the wall. Even when Dick came down beside her, she did not try to say anything. She gave a little sob as he put his arms around her.

"Can you hold on around my neck?" Dick asked, and she reached up her arms obediently. He braced her against his knee and called to Jerry:

"Up-Up."

His voice echoed and re-echoed in the narrow hole. Suppose Jerry couldn't hear, suppose he didn't understand. But the rope tightened and lifted. The sound of the creaking windlass came echoing down. Betsey in her wet clothes was unexpectedly heavy. He began to think she might slip out of his arms. How lucky it was that she was so quiet; if she had struggled at all, they would have been dashed against the slimy stone walls. The round light above was like a moon, like a cartwheel. The chilly air began to feel warm and dry

again; they were up. Jerry had hold of them both and had lifted them out. Betsey burst suddenly into a storm of tears.

"Mother told me not to step on the well and I forgot," she wailed.

Jerry had taken her in his arms and was walking up and down with her, quieting her as though she was a baby. Dick lay down on the grass, warm, sweet dry grass and shut his eyes for a minute. He could hear feet running; the Usher family had heard Jerry's shouts and were almost down the hill. Fleet-footed Nora got to them first.

Mrs. Usher was taking her little daughter out of Jerry's arms, but she was looking across Betsey's wet red curls at Dick, where he had sat up, still feeling dizzy and wondering if it had really happened. The look Sara Usher gave him, of joy, of thankfulness for Betsey, of gratitude to him, of real love, was something that did not need any words to go with it. There was true beauty in that worn face, so changed now under relief and happiness. They all went up to the house together, Dick walking between Nora and Sam. He felt a little unsteady, it was good to have them near.

He got quite as much attention as Betsey did, he remembered afterward. Sam took him into his tiny room and gave him some clothes of his own, helped to rub him dry, rubbed his hair until it was all standing on end. Mrs. Usher made him drink a cup of steaming hot tea. But he was in a perfect glow and did not need it. Suddenly everybody was talking, all of them together and Betsey, quite cheerful again, was in the middle of them all and was saying over and over, "But it was dark down there just like in the night."

One thing was very clear, there was no use in thinking that Dick and Jerry could ask Mrs. Usher any of the questions that were in their minds. They got up therefore and went out to Jerry's car. Mrs. Usher was still hovering over little Betsey, she seemed hardly to notice that they were going. The others stood there in the sun while the two got in and Jerry started the engine. "I'm going to send the doctor up to have a look at Betsey," he said, "though she certainly seems all right." Mr. Usher was struggling to say something, and not succeeding very well. Jerry lifted up his hand. "Don't try to say it, we know," he declared. "We'll see you soon. So long."

As they went swiftly down the hill, Dick spoke only once. "Do you remember that day last autumn when I saw you first?" Jerry nodded. "And you said that living in the country was different and things would happen I wasn't used to. They do, don't they?"

"Yes," Jerry answered. "They do."

They came up to the big house, the doors and windows were all open and they could hear Mother singing in the kitchen. The girls were playing out under the trees and Roddy was thumping away at his printing press in the cellar. The two friends stood on the threshold, hesitating a minute.

"I am the one to tell your mother," Jerry said. "She

may never let me come into this house again, when she knows that it was I who sent you down the well."

"I was wondering how I could get down it, myself," Dick insisted. They went out to Mother in the kitchen.

She heard Jerry's story. She had to sit down suddenly on the kitchen stool when he got to the main part, but she went on listening without a word. She gave Dick a look of love and pride, and she had just such another one for Jerry when he had finished.

"And Betsey was really all right?" she asked anxiously. "How good, how very good that her mother did not see her go down. And all that you and Dick did was exactly what you should do. I would have been ashamed if he had not gone to help her." But Dick saw that she had turned pale at the very thought of what they had had to do.

Jerry must stay for lunch, Mother insisted it was almost ready. Jerry was very willing. "If he feels as tired out as I do," Dick was thinking, "he will be glad just to sit here and not go home for awhile." Before they had finished Mrs. Towner had come running over, across the grass to the back door.

"I've just heard," she said. "No, I won't stop in and disturb you." She spoke in a loud whisper that could easily be heard well into the dining room. "Bless the boy, bless them both."

To Dick's relief she went home without coming in to exclaim and ask questions. But he saw her stop someone outside as she was going home, and that someone went hastening down into the village, full of news.

The sun had gone in, this was not a summer day after all, only the pretense of one. A chilly wind had sprung up and it began to rain, drearily and steadily, not the sort that would make floods and excitement, only the sort that made everything dark and damp and dull. Dick could not settle to anything, and as the excitement finally went out of him he felt shamefully idle and dreary. He noticed that Jerry was only pretending to read the newspaper as he waited for the showers to clear. They did not clear.

Suddenly Jerry looked up. "There's somebody coming up to the door," he said to Dick. "Why it's the Ushers, Mr. and Mrs. Usher at least." The little car had indeed come to the front steps and stopped with a gulp and a gasp.

Mr. and Mrs. Usher came in, they looked strange in their dark clothes which must be their best ones. Dick had never seen them before in anything but overalls and aprons. Mother came in to greet them. She opened the door into the big parlor and drew out chairs from beside the table. There was something on their faces that made Dick know that this was not just a visit to say thank you, or we are glad your boy is all right. There was something more, even more than that. Mrs. Usher finally managed to speak.

"It's a little matter of business," she said. Her voice was thin and a trifle high.

Her husband cleared his throat. "It's something Sara, my wife, wanted to tell you about. I didn't know about it myself until an hour ago. She was quite right, saying we mustn't wait to tell you. But she has waited a long time."

"Mr. Styles, I thought he ought to hear it too," Mrs. Usher said. She hadn't sat down although Jerry had put a chair for her. "Do you think we might go over to his office?"

"I'll telephone to see if he is there," Mother said and went out. She came back in a minute. "He says it will be quicker if he comes over," she told them. "He will be here at once." Mrs. Usher sat down then, she had a shabby black bag on her arm and she put it carefully on her lap. Her husband sat by her; Jerry pulled up a chair and motioned to Dick to sit beside him. Mother had a look of puzzled wonder on her face, but she did not ask any questions. The big room was very still while they waited. They could hear Roddy's printing press below. The rain splashed the windows and splashed again.

Mr. Styles had hurried so he was breathless, and came up the steps shaking the drops out of his big umbrella. But he seemed very calm, as he sat down at the head of the table, taking charge of things. "Now Mrs. Usher, if you will explain to us what it was we ought to hear," he began.

She was not very good at explaining, she kept getting mixed up and having to begin over again. But everyone was patient and quiet and Mr. Styles' questions led her forward in what she had to say.

"Your father, Mrs. Milton, came to our house on that last day before he was taken sick. He had bought the farm where we lived, you know that, and we were wondering whether he would be willing to have us stay on. I — was very upset, thinking he might not."

"Yes," said Jerry. "That was Maria Malvern's doing, you needn't explain."

"My husband was in the barn, so Mr. Devons just said to me that he would want us to sign some papers about the farm. I thought — " she stopped and choked, "I thought that meant for sure that he wanted us to go. That was all he said, and he went out to the barn to speak to my husband. They got to talking about some new beams for the roof, though, and Mr. Devons never said anything more about papers. He took off his coat and they measured off together what timbers were going to be needed. Then Mr. Devons went home."

She stopped, and Mr. Usher moved a little in his chair and put his hand on her arm. It seemed to give her courage so she went on. "We heard, a little while after, that Mr. Devons got sick that night, and in a few days that he was gone. Everyone sorrowed for him, he was surely a good man."

Mr. Styles turned to Mother. "You might have wondered whether that journey up the hill that day was the cause of your father's illness. The doctor told me that it wasn't, his trouble was something that might have come on him any time or anywhere. Mr. Devons seemed to have something on his mind, the doctor said. He kept saying that he had an errand at the bank. But he couldn't make it clear what it was. Now Mrs. Usher — "

"It was weeks, no it was months later; Rob Dale and I were in the barn. He was helping that day. It was he who found the papers that had fallen out of Mr. Devons's pocket — they had got under the hay. Rob gave them to me. I thought — I thought — " tears were coming but she managed to go on. "I thought of course they were papers about our giving up the farm. I thought if anyone else saw they would know Mr. Devons had meant us to leave. I — I just couldn't show them."

Jerry Stewart moved his chair to come around and sit on the other side of her. "It's all right," he said quietly. "Everything is all right. Just go on. So you kept the package of papers? Did you ever think they might be — something else?"

"No, never." she sounded surprised. "I just thought they were about the farm. The envelope was pasted shut, and Mr. Devons had written his own name on the outside. I couldn't even dare to open it and look. So I just kept them — until now."

She opened the bag on her lap and took out a long envelope. She pushed it across the table and Mr. Styles put his hand on it, but no more than that.

"What made you bring it now, today?" he asked gently. "Was it because of little Betsey being rescued from the well?"

"That was the last of it," she said. "But it was much more that brought me to it. Mrs. Milton was kind, kind like her father, and I stopped a little being afraid. And her children were such good friends with my children. And it was, most of all, seeing how they were, all of them, as a family, how they stood by each other and didn't ask favors of anyone, how they just went on their way, never complained that people in the town weren't — just friendly — seemed to think they oughtn't to have the house."

Mother spoke very suddenly. "The people in the village were quite right. If it had been true that my father lost Jerry's money, of course we oughtn't to have the house. The people couldn't help showing what they thought, and what they thought was really quite fair, if the money had been gone."

Mr. Styles asked exactly what Jerry had asked a minute ago. "Did you never think that these papers might have been something else?"

Mrs. Usher shook her head, she couldn't say any more. Dick could see that Mother was breathing fast and that Mr. Styles' long hand was pressed down hard on the envelope. Only Jerry did not seem to be excited. He gave Mrs. Usher a kind and quiet look. She was crying openly now. Mr. Styles pushed the envelope across to Jerry Stewart.

"You're the one to open it," he said. Jerry shook his head. "No, Dick," he insisted, and it was Dick who slit the envelope and pulled out a handful of very heavy papers with greenish printing on them. He pushed them back to Mr. Styles who picked them up, one by one.

"Bonds," Andrew Styles said. "Four government bonds of five thousand dollars each. Made out in your

name, Jerry. That was what Roger Devons did with
your money; brought it from $15,000 up to $20,000
and then put it into government bonds at last for safe
keeping. He seems to have bought them through some
agent that he used in New York," he added, "so the
records didn't go through the bank here. But that was
only a chance. He evidently was going to put them
into the bank that day. I think that he never knew
that he dropped them." He pushed back his chair
and his face was shining with happiness. "There's
always an answer," he said, "and you see the doubts and
suspicious thoughts fly away and there's the truth left."

"And they aren't about the farm?" Mrs. Usher cried
out. The color had come back to her face and she had
stopped crying.

It was Mother who answered. "Not about the farm
at all. And you can be sure that you can live there as
long as I am alive and my children are."

The Ushers got up to go. Mrs. Usher looked con-
fused, as though she still did not quite understand, but
Mr. Usher's face was glowing like Mr. Styles'. Andrew
Styles went with them to the door for a last word.
Jerry smiled across at Mother and Dick.

"So you don't have to give me a house," he said.
"I am anxious to know what you will do, now that
you feel that it is really yours." Mother answered
quickly.

"When the children's father was here we talked it
all out, what we would do if the house was ours, what
we would do if it wasn't. We have saved a good deal

of money by living here and doing everything ourselves, so we think by the end of the summer we could
go to South America for a short visit. When we get to
Chile it will be just the beginning of spring."

Dick had to think twice about that. He had forgotten
that lower South America was, as Roddy once said,
"the upside down of New England."

"But we will come back for the next school year,
since we do not know when my husband will be ordered
elsewhere. And we will always come back, in summers
and other times. We may still have to wander all
over the world to follow their father's work, but we
will have something of our own, that we can think of as
home, as the place where our good friends are."

Roddy had come upstairs and now wandered in
through the hall, to find out what everybody was
doing. "What did the Ushers want?" he asked. Dick
told him, quickly and in much excitement. But Roddy
got the idea. "We know where the money went? Jerry
has it again." He stood stunned for a long minute
and then burst out —

"I'll put it in my paper, I'll just say that Mrs. Usher
found the money. We'll get out an extra. I was going
have one about Betsey Usher, but everybody knows
about that now. Nobody knows about this, they won't
until they read it in the *Jefferson Journal*. Come and
help me, Dick."

A nod from Mother was enough. The two boys
dashed across the hall and went running down the
basement stairs.